Rush

Also by Robin Covington

A NIGHT OF SOUTHERN COMFORT
HIS SOUTHERN TEMPTATION
SWEET SOUTHERN BETRAYAL
PLAYING THE PART
SEX & THE SINGLE VAMP
PLAYING WITH THE DRUMMER
DARING THE PLAYER
TEMPTATION
SALVATION
REDEMPTION
THE PRINCE'S RUNAWAY LOVER
ONE LITTLE KISS
SECRET SANTA BABY

Rush
By Robin Covington

A MacKenzie Family Novella

Introduction by Liliana Hart

EVIL EYE
CONCEPTS

Rush
A MacKenzie Family Novella
Copyright 2016 by Robin Covington d/b/a Burning Up the Sheets, LLC.
ISBN: 978-1-942299-39-4

Published by Evil Eye Concepts, Incorporated

Introduction copyright 2016 Liliana Hart

Acknowledgments

Special thanks to Liliana Hart for asking me to be part of this project and for being a friend.

Hugs to Liz Berry and MJ Rose for being so wonderful to work with and making this such a blast.

A shout out to Christopher Rice, Cristin Harber, Avery Flynn, and Kimberly Kincaid for stepping up my game. Yeah…I'm fangirling a little bit over here.

To the Main Man, Little Man and Lulu – huge hugs and kisses for your unwavering support. How blessed am I to get to spend my days and nights with you?

An Introduction to the MacKenzie Family World

Dear Readers,

I'm thrilled to be able to introduce the MacKenzie Family World to you. I asked five of my favorite authors to create their own characters and put them into the world you all know and love. These amazing authors revisited Surrender, Montana, and through their imagination you'll get to meet new characters, while reuniting with some of your favorites.

These stories are hot, hot, hot—exactly what you'd expect from a MacKenzie story—and it was pure pleasure for me to read each and every one of them and see my world through someone else's eyes. They definitely did the series justice, and I hope you discover five new authors to put on your auto-buy list.

Make sure you check out *Troublemaker*, a brand new, full-length MacKenzie novel written by me. And yes, you'll get to see more glimpses of Shane before his book comes out next year.

So grab a glass of wine, pour a bubble bath, and prepare to Surrender.

Love Always,

Liliana Hart

Available now!

Trouble Maker by Liliana Hart
Rush by Robin Covington
Bullet Proof by Avery Flynn
Delta: Rescue by Cristin Harber
Deep Trouble by Kimberly Kincaid
Desire & Ice by Christopher Rice

Chapter One

"You've got five seconds to get the fuck off my property or I will bury you on it."

Atticus Rush had zero patience for people who just showed up on his doorstep. Sure, he should probably give the trespassers props for finding him lodged deep in the heart of nowhere Montana, but he couldn't muster up the enthusiasm when he resented the hell out of their very existence.

And he deeply resented the large man currently standing on his porch.

He'd tracked the truck coming up the long driveway, watching as they pulled into the yard under his trees and cut the engine. Uneasy when anyone showed up at his house uninvited, he'd exited his house through the back door and then circled around the side yard and waited in the bushes as the unwelcome trespasser got out of the vehicle and mounted the front porch steps. As the man rang the bell, Rush had silently crept up behind him and pressed the muzzle of his gun to the back of the man's head. His visitor had raised his hands in the air without being told.

"Dammit, Rush. Put the gun down. If you kill me, Darcy will be royally pissed off."

The voice was familiar, friendly, so he lowered the gun a little bit and used his free hand to nudge the man around. One look at his face and Rush engaged the safety on the weapon and lowered the muzzle to face the ground. Brant Scott wasn't exactly *unwelcome* but if he was here unannounced, it wasn't a good thing.

"Scott, what did you do? Join the Jehovah's Witnesses or something?" he asked as he shouldered his way past his old friend to get to the door.

"What are you talking about?"

"Being hit by the sudden urge to save my eternal soul is the only thing I can think of that would make you come here without letting me know first."

"We both know you don't have a soul to save."

Unable to argue with such blatant truth, Rush pressed his palm against the lock pad and shoved the door open to get inside. He strode across the stone floor of the entryway and entered the large open space housing the kitchen and living room. The back wall was almost entirely made of glass, the view of the mountain range behind the house the only rival for the attention normally commanded by the two-story stone fireplace.

Sliding the clip out of his gun, he placed them both on the counter, reached into the fridge and emerged with a solitary beer. Brant leaned against the island and stared at him with narrow eyes as he took a long, deep swallow.

"What?" he asked, wiping his mouth with the back of his hand, glaring across the kitchen.

"You're not going to offer me a beer?"

"Are we going to pretend this is a social call?"

The stare-down continued for a few long moments and Rush took another swig of beer before Brant broke first and advanced forward, jerking the door to the fridge open with a curse. Rush barely bit back a sharp bite of laughter as he watched him slam the door and viciously pop the cap off the bottle.

"How long are you going to bust my balls?" Brant asked on a swallow and then pointed at him across the island. "You could have blown my head off, asshole."

"It's my land. My porch. I'm sure you saw the multitude of *No Trespassing* signs I posted." He shrugged. "You trespass and I shoot you. Seems like a very easy concept to grasp."

"No wonder you live out here in the middle of nowhere. Nobody can stand you," Brant grumbled, giving him the evil eye. "And what the fuck is up with your hair?"

At that, Rush did let a small laugh get past his lips. Seeing the usually collected Brant lose his shit even just a little bit was fun. The only person that could get him ruffled was his wife, Darcy. That was fun to watch too. Or at least it was until they started with the kissy-kissy love crap. That's when he usually made himself scarce and high-tailed it back to his mountain.

"It's long," he answered, shrugging off Brant's skeptical raised eyebrow. "I have no problem catching tail with it."

Brant stared at him, lifting his hand to make an "anything else" movement with his fingers. "That's it?"

"Is there anything else?" Brant opened his mouth and Rush could almost hear the lecture about how "great marriage was with the right woman." Blah. Blah. Blah. He was not the marrying kind...not again, at any rate. The women he met for occasional weekends to blow off steam were fine when his right hand and Astroglide weren't cutting it any longer. Marriage? Once burned, twice shy...or something like that. He'd risked his heart once and he wouldn't do it again. "Are we at the point where you stop pretending that you're here because you missed me?"

Brant eyed him across the short distance, clearly weighing whether he would go through with what he'd come here to do. Rush waited him out, but each passing second convinced him that this was not a proposal he was going to like.

"MacKenzie Security needs your help." He paused as he pulled his phone out of his jeans pocket. "*I* need your help."

He thumbed the screen and tapped a couple of times before turning it to face Rush. A young girl, smiling huge and hugging a Labrador Retriever. She was about twelve years old and she looked familiar. *Very familiar.*

He put down his beer on the counter and reached out for the phone, pulling back at the last minute. He looked at Brant.

"I know her."

"You do," he answered with a nod. "That is Katrina Hickman. Senator Alan Hickman's daughter. You met her four years ago when the president pinned another medal on your chest." Brant's voice took on the cadence of a very patient teacher who would keep adding facts until the student understood the lesson. "She was at the ceremony and followed you around the entire time. She had quite a crush on you, as I recall. Was devastated when you showed up with a bride six months later."

Boom. All the memories came back like a wave. He *did* remember her.

"She was cute. Loved telling awful knock-knock jokes. She wrote me for a year, included drawings in the letters." He swallowed hard, already dreading the reason why Brant was holding up her picture. "What happened to her?"

"Someone took her this morning."

Rage replaced the dread and coated his veins in ice. Katrina's attention had embarrassed him at times; her crush was obvious to anyone who saw how she looked at him. He'd tiptoed around the minefield of little-girl feelings and worked hard to make sure she didn't get the wrong impression. In spite of his best intentions, his marriage to Livvy had broken Katrina's heart.

The thought of her in the hands of anyone who might hurt her was goddam unacceptable.

"When? How?" He barked out the questions.

"All I know is that she was on her way to school and they took her on the sidewalk. Disabled her security so effectively we can't discount an inside job. They left a note in the guard's pocket stating they would call later with their demands."

"So why do you need me? You've got an entire security firm at your disposal."

"The senator asked for you."

Oh fuck no. He reached out and minimized the photo on the screen and pushed it back toward Brant. He'd promised to never do any more work for that man. Yeah, he was a mercenary but he had his principles and Hickman violated all of them.

"Put your guys on it. I don't do this anymore."

Brant's snort was derisive. "Really? You don't sell your skills to the highest bidder? Navy SEAL for sale. Throw enough money at him and he'll ignore how dirty you are or…"

Rush moved fast and Brant was spun around and slammed against the fridge before they could take another breath. It was no small feat to get the jump on Brant. He was highly skilled but Rush was bigger at six feet five inches and had about forty pounds on him. He pressed his forearm against Brant's throat, enough to make it hard for him to talk, enough to make him rethink the next words out of his mouth.

"Listen, I don't need to justify to you how I make my living. I'm very selective. *I* get to choose. Which is a hell of a lot more choice than I got when I worked for the senator."

"You worked for Hickman? Doing what?" Brant's expression was clouded with confusion, his fingers pulling at Rush's arm until he relented and loosened his grip. They both backed away, staring each other down across the kitchen. Rush racked his brain for what he could tell him. What came out was true but trite.

"That's classified."

Brant gave that two beats before he nodded. "Classified?" He ran a hand over his face in exasperation. "Rush, what the hell have you been doing since you left the Navy?"

"You really don't want to know."

The silence stretched out between them and Rush exhaled slowly when Brant turned toward the front door, but his breath caught in his chest when his friend grabbed the phone off the counter and thumbed it on again. The screen lit up with Katrina's smiling face.

Her innocent face. Her father was an ass and quite possibly a criminal, but she was just a kid. It was like Brant could read his mind.

"She's just a kid, Rush. We don't know who took her or where she is but you and I both know that if we aren't prepared to act when we get the demands, death will be the lesser of many evils. Our intel says her father has been dealing with people who make young girls disappear and make a tidy profit at the same time. A young white woman with her pedigree would be a prize and you know it."

He didn't need to be told the horrible things that could happen to a pretty girl these days.

And yes, death would be the least of these.

He had no choice. Not really. He was a dick but he wasn't heartless. But he also wasn't stupid and he had his own demands.

"I want you, Elena, Jade, and two more of your best guys. If they have ex-fil experience, that would be ideal. I won't have time to train any newbies on this field trip." He moved past Brant, headed back to his office to gather the equipment he'd need. "No commercial flights. I need to take some shit that would ensure both of us getting multiple cavity searches from TSA. I don't mind a little ass play but not from a ham-fisted guy named Bob at the security checkpoint."

Brant followed close behind and Rush grabbed a duffel bag and moved toward his weapons safe, keying in the code and yanking the door open when the lock released.

"How fast can we get to the location? I'll need scans of the area, topography, plans of the structure. You know the drill."

Brant's voice was low. "We don't know where she's being held."

"What?" Rush stopped his inventory of ammo and guns. "It's going to be hard for me to get her out if I don't know where she is. My specialty is extraction."

"Understood. We're short on time, so we need someone who can find anything...or anyone."

"And?" Brant did that look-away thing again and Rush tensed, his gut telling him he already knew what was coming.

"We need you to ask *her* for help." Rush didn't have to ask the obvious question. "We need you to ask Olivia to help us out on this one."

"No. You've got to find someone on your staff to find Katrina."

"My best guy is out-of-pocket and I don't have time to pull him back. I would never ask you to contact her if it wasn't important."

Rush bowed his head, his heartbeat loud and rapid in his ears. It was the sudden rise in his blood pressure, the twist in his gut, and the stab in a spot under his left ribs. He looked down at his hands, white-knuckled with a slight tremor where they clasped the magazine full of bullets.

She still got to him and Brant knew it, knew what he was asking. He was one of the few people who did. Too much tequila on a ski trip and Rush had spilled his guts, telling the story of how a gutter kid from Baltimore had reached too high and fallen for the prom queen. The girl from the rightest of right side of the tracks, complete with generations of sterling silver spoons in her mouth and a title...several of them, actually.

Lady Olivia Rutledge-Cairn.

His Livvy.

For a brief time also known as Mrs. Atticus Rush.

And known to a very few as "Irene Adler"—a name given to her by a charmed Interpol agent who had failed to catch her half a dozen times. As the world's most infamous modern-day thief, she was uniquely qualified to find the location of anything of great value, including a young girl.

Rush knew she could do it. She'd stolen his heart and he'd never gotten it back. She was *that* fucking good.

Goddamn, he'd loved her. He hadn't known he was capable until she walked into his life on her ridiculously expensive high heels.

"I can't ask her, Brant. She won't do it for me." He was about to say that the divorce had been ugly but really, it hadn't. He'd found out who she was. She left. He filed. She didn't fight it. It was final on their one-year anniversary. And three years later, he was still reeling from the body blow.

But maybe she wasn't. All indicators were that she'd moved on. New lovers. New thefts. Her usual jet-set lifestyle of parties and vacations on private islands. If there was ever a reason to test the waters of how deep her hatred ran, this was the time.

"Fine. I'll ask her." He resumed placing the weaponry in the specially designed duffel, his mind already calculating the hours lapsed, the time to travel, and when they could expect the first call from the kidnappers. They didn't have a ton of time to fuck around. "Try to get in touch with your guy just in case Olivia isn't up to playing nice or shoots me on sight. I'll be ready to go in ten minutes and your pilot needs to file an expedited international flight plan."

Brant was nodding, already dialing his phone when he looked up. "International?"

"Yeah. Olivia is in Mexico."

"You know where your ex-wife is at this very moment?"

He laughed and didn't try to disguise the bitter edge to the sound. "Marriage to Livvy taught me that knowing where she is at all times is a *very good* thing."

Chapter Two

She didn't recognize the car in her driveway.

SUV. Rental. She wasn't expecting any guests.

Olivia didn't quicken her pace. This was her favorite time of the day, strolling the quiet streets of the waterfront Mexican village where she kept one of her several homes. July in Mexico probably wasn't most people's ideal time to visit, but an early lifetime of England's soft rain and mild summers caused a bone-deep craving for the hottest of days. Heat that penetrated down to her marrow made her feel alive, vibrant, happy.

The breeze from the ocean swept up the back of her dress and ruffled her hair as she mounted the steps and turned the latch on the gate. Inside the walled courtyard the air was cooler, the shade deeper, and the smell of flowering tropical plants almost overpowering. She followed the sound of voices to the seating area, wondering if she'd forgotten an appointment.

"Matilda, I'm home," she called out, rounding the corner with a curious smile on her lips.

She should have done something cliché, like dropping her straw tote and spilling the fruit, vegetables, and fish across the terra cotta paving stones. At the very least she should have teetered on her high-heeled sandals, had to grab the chair to keep herself steady. But she didn't do any of that.

She was Lady Olivia Rutledge-Cairn, only daughter of the Earl and Countess of Lisdale, and she damn well knew how to keep her cool when a ghost appeared on her patio.

Even if the ghost was Atticus Rush.

A large, dark, brooding specter rising from the burial ground of her heart, their volatile love and disastrous marriage. Time had changed him a little. There were more lines around his eyes, and a long, nasty scar on his forearm that hadn't been there three years ago dissected one of his favorite tattoos. The full beard and mustache was new but suited him. But the biggest change was the dark mane of hair, pulled back with a leather thong and ending just below his shoulder blades. It was the polar opposite from the severe Navy-issued "high and tight" he'd worn when they'd met.

"Atticus, what the bloody hell did you do to your hair?" It slipped out before she could stop herself.

The man beside him snickered and Olivia recognized that he was Brant Scott, an old friend of her ex-husband. He'd been on the list of people to call if she'd needed help when Atticus was deployed.

"Why the fuck is everyone so concerned about my hair?" Atticus growled as he pulled his hands out of his pockets and crossed his arms over his chest. The heated glower on his face, combined with the hostile stance, reminded her of stories of marauding Norsemen depicted in some of the old tapestries covering the walls of her childhood home.

"You look like a Viking ready to plunder the shores," she said, hoping her tone was lighter than she felt inside. Gut tight, heart pounding, mouth dry, she had to clutch her fingers tightly around the handles of her tote to keep from taking the few steps between them and kissing him or something equally insane.

"I won't be invading any Saxon territory today," he said, his tone less grumpy but devoid of any soft or suggestive innuendo. She took his words at face value. Whatever brought him here, it wasn't the sudden urge to reconcile.

Olivia swallowed down the regret-soaked lump in her throat and turned to the thing she could do in her sleep and in any state of disappointment: hospitality.

"Well, then..." She turned and handed her bag to her housekeeper with a smile. "Matilda, the invaders come in peace. Can you bring out some cool refreshments?" She approached the man standing beside Atticus, leaning up to accept his kiss on her cheek. "Brant, it's wonderful to see you."

"You too, Olivia." He smiled back at her but it faltered when he shifted back, glanced over, and left a clear path toward her other guest.

She stood still, waiting for a cue from her ex-husband on how this would go. It was awkward when you went from knowing every intimate detail of each other's bodies to people who only spoke through their attorneys. They both stared at each other for a moment and then she remembered that the last time she'd seen Atticus she'd been the one to blink first and this wasn't going to be a repeat. She waited him out, only letting out her breath when he spoke.

"You look good," he observed in a gruff tone. The brusque compliment was accompanied by a brief nod in her direction. There was no move to touch her or close the distance. It was... disappointing, but she'd never let it show.

"Thank you," she said and covered up her nerves with taking over serving the refreshments delivered to the table. Olivia motioned for them to sit as she offered up the icy drinks. "Tea? Beer? Iced coffee?"

"You drink cold tea?" Brant asked, indicating his choice of beverage.

"Have you noticed how hot it is? I'm British, not insane." Olivia turned to Atticus, handing over the iced coffee she knew he would prefer. Actually, he'd want black, hot coffee but the thought of being within five feet of a steaming urn of anything made her cringe. Their fingers brushed but she was ready for it, schooling her features to disguise the leap of her heart and the full-body shiver at the contact.

Atticus did jump a little, enough for her to tell, and she smiled a the grin growing wider when he glowered and placed his glass on the table without taking a sip.

"You're not thirsty? I can get you..."

"This isn't a social call, Olivia," Atticus said. "We need your help."

His tone was hard, urgent—in total contrast to the softer plea in both his and Brant's eyes. Whatever this was, it was serious, and her own fingers stalled over the drink tray.

"Well, let's get to it then."

Brant began. "Katrina Hickman, a twelve-year-old girl, was kidnapped this morning in front of her school. We need you to help us find out where she's been taken." He glanced at Atticus. "He is going to lead the extraction team once we locate her but we have no leads about her location."

"I'm very sorry to hear this but I don't see…"

Atticus cut her off. His tone was even but she could feel the urgency coming off him in waves. She wanted to get up and put her hands on him, soothe him. In some way this was personal for him.

"We think this could be retaliation against her father, Senator Alan Hickman. My guess is he's been hanging out with dangerous men, the kind who have no qualms killing a young girl or doing much worse."

She flinched. She knew what "worse" meant.

Brant joined in. "Your connections, your skill set, your ability to locate things on legitimate and illegitimate markets are what we need right now. This is a very short fuse and Hickman is hiding things from us. We're going to have to fight dirty to get the intel we need to save this girl."

She scanned them both, trying to process the information. Yes, she was very good at locating items—especially items that were not on legitimate markets. Her connections around the globe gave her contacts to people who dwelled in the light of day and in the underworld. And yes…she had the gift of taking things. She did see it as a gift; her mind could assess a scene, take apart the puzzle of access, alarms, and security, and then flawlessly and seamlessly remove the item and disappear into the night.

How Brant knew that she did all those things would be a topic for another day. Apparently her usually close-lipped ex-husband had confided in this man and spilled her secrets.

"MacKenzie Security has a plethora of employees who can do what I do. Why not use them?"

"My people are in places where I can't get them back in time," he said.

She turned her gaze to Atticus. "This is acceptable to you? Our working together?"

"You know Katrina Hickman, Livvy. She was the young girl

who sent me the drawings when we were... together." He stumbled over the word and her throat tightened with the impact of his vulnerability. "The one who you said—"

"...made me feel like the other woman." Suddenly it all came back to her. A small, blond-haired girl who worshipped Atticus with an adoration that made your heart ache with its sincerity. She'd been sweet, so lovely. Olivia had liked her, recognizing a girl who was dying for some attention and affection from her own experience. "Oh no, not her."

His dark eyes locked on hers and this time she couldn't suppress the shiver. He was clearly upset by this situation—who wouldn't be?—but this was also personal for him. She could feel his anxious pain just under the surface of his skin, see it in his eyes.

If he'd remained cold and distant she could have agreed with no hesitation, but the pain in his gaze over this girl cut her to the quick. His ability to shut down completely had been something she'd gotten used to during their brief marriage. So, it was the rare glimpses of his huge heart, his massive capacity to care about something that rocked her world.

Even if a sweet little girl hadn't been in danger, she'd have done it for that look alone.

"I need to pack a few things. I can be ready to go in twenty minutes."

"Great," Brant said, rising from his seat and grabbing his cell phone out of his pocket. "I'll call the pilot and get us cleared to leave."

He walked away, his phone pressed to his ear as he gave directions. Atticus stared at her across the table, his expression as difficult to read as always.

"Say *something*, Atticus." How many times had she said that during their time together? "I know this wasn't your idea."

"No. It wasn't." He stood, rolling his shoulders as if he could shake off the tension weighing down the air between them like a humid veil. "But Brant is right. You are the best for this job."

She rose to her feet, walking over to him. He was much too tall for her to look him directly in the eye but with her heels on, she didn't have to crane her neck to at least gaze at his chin. He turned and she fought the impulse to step backward. They were closer than she'd planned but she wasn't going to be the one to yield ground.

"This isn't a trick, is it?"

"What?" His eyes searched her face, his expression of confusion a welcome change from the glowering he'd done since he'd arrived.

"This isn't a ploy to get me back in DC and turn me over to the FBI?"

"What? No."

His hand wrapped around her arm, pulling her close. She could feel the warmth of his breath on her cheek, the brush of his hair against her bare shoulder. She swayed on her heels a little, enough to cause her to reach out and grasp his hip for balance.

"You can't blame me for asking," she said. "The last time we were in the same room together you planned to turn me in."

He inhaled sharply. "You have my word."

"Do I?" His eyes narrowed at her question, not liking the fact that she'd questioned him. Well, that was just too bad. "Do I?"

She leaned up before she knew what she was going to do, shock racing over her skin and causing goose bumps when their lips met. It was barely a brush of skin on skin, the heat of their breaths slickening the slow glide of their lips. It wasn't until she did it that she realized how much she'd missed it, wanted it.

Olivia pulled away, backing completely out of his zone.

"Why did you do that?" he asked, his body turning away slightly as if he needed even more distance between them.

She said the first thing that came to her mind, the truth of the matter. There was no honor among thieves but Atticus had his own personal code and it was unbreakable.

"With our past, this bargain had to be sealed with a kiss."

He let out a sharp bark of taut laughter, the first hint of a smile, and she responded in kind. When he did that, she couldn't fail to respond. It had gotten her in trouble with him before. She needed to be careful. "Judas betrayed with a kiss, Livvy."

She gave him a long, lingering look before turning toward the house. She needed to pack clothes and her tools.

"You might be many things, Atticus Rush, but you are no Judas."

Chapter Three

Rush really hated pretentious pricks.

He didn't like many people, period, but he really despised pretentious pricks.

Senator Hickman was the pretentious prick that every up-and-coming prick in Washington, DC aspired to be. He was also a criminal and had a morality that was so far into the darkness it resembled those weird mutant fish that existed in the depths of the ocean. Blind and oddly colored like C-4 explosive.

A bottom dweller. That's what Hickman was. And if it wasn't for an innocent young girl, he would've kept his promise to never do anything for him again.

"Mr. Scott." The senator rose from behind his desk and extended his hand to Brant. The office was huge, decorated in "early presidential aspiration" and spanned almost the entire width of his expensive DC townhouse. "Thank you and MacKenzie Security for handling this for me."

Brant shook his hand, his own smile equally fake and tight. "As I told you, our firm is booked with other missions but I've brought on the best to lead in the rescue of Katrina." He motioned to Rush. "I know you're familiar with Rush."

The senator stilled, his face losing all trace of civility. The cold, harsh expression on his face was the real deal and when you saw it, you realized that the other was a mask. Unfortunately enough people were fooled that he kept getting reelected.

"Is he the best you can do, Scott?" the senator asked, his voice loud and ugly. He was obviously going to act like he hadn't requested for Rush to do this for him. He couldn't even be straight up when his daughter's life was on the line.

"He's *the best*," Brant said and Rush got tired of being only the subject of this conversation.

He advanced into the room, his heavy boots thumping loudly on the hardwood floors. They all turned to face him—Brant frustrated at his failure to follow directions to make nice with the assholes and Hickman's face flushed an angry red. Rush stopped in the middle of the room, arms crossed and eyes sharp.

"I'd love to keep discussing how big my dick is but we've got a little girl to save and *you asked* for me because I'm the one to get it done. So, why don't we cut all the bullshit and you tell me who you've been playing with, Alan? What dirty pig have you been rolling in the mud with and what did you do to put your daughter at risk?"

"You can't talk to me like that," Hickman fumed.

"I don't look like I'm in uniform anymore, do I?" Rush looked down at his clothes and back up with a smirk on his face. "I can talk to you any way I want."

"Gentleman, we have a young girl who needs our help. Do we need to whip them out and measure or can we just move on? I'm sure I have a little ruler in my purse." Livvy walked right into the middle of the testosterone circle and stared them all down, one by one. Dressed all in black—high heels with a sexy ankle strap, dressy short-shorts, and a top that slipped down and exposed a creamy shoulder—she was pretty fucking magnificent. She stuck out her hand for Hickman.

"Lady Olivia Rutledge-Cairn," she said, casting her eyes in a slow circle around the room, her smile sweet with a hint of wicked. "I'm here to help in any way—"

She tripped and lurched forward into Hickman. He reached out and caught her, his disgust morphing into a leer and hands wandering in dangerous proximity to her ass. Rush growled and Livvy laughed and scooted out of grope range while still sending out a "catch me if you can" vibe. He didn't like it. Not one fucking bit. Every part of him screamed that she was his but he had a court issued document that said otherwise.

"I'm so sorry. These heels are ridiculous." She swept her hand down toward her mile-long legs and Hickman was too busy ogling to notice her slip his phone into her purse. He knew the remote cloning device located inside the bag was now sending the contents of the phone to Elena for retrieval and dissection. Damn, she was good. He could almost forget that her life's vocation was taking things that belonged to other people. "Could we sit down?"

"Yes, of course," Hickman said, making sure he got the seat next to her on the loveseat and moving in close. Asshole. His daughter was missing, his wife was likely doped on a pill the doc gave her, and he was trying to cop a feel. Rush remained standing. "My condolences on the death of your father. The earl was a great friend of the United States."

Livvy bit her bottom lip, her one tell about her emotions when something upset her. She'd been close to her father, their age difference making him more like a grandfather. While her mother had lived the jet-set life with lovers in Monte Carlo, her older brothers had largely ignored her and she been raised by the staff when allowed to be at home and not shipped off to boarding school. He'd sent flowers to the service, their only communication post-divorce, and he still had the short note of thanks she'd sent him. Rush shook off the memory, getting his head back in the game.

"Thank you, but we're here to get Katrina back." Livvy shifted the conversation back to the point with no hint of censure in her voice. She was good at the diplomacy thing.

"Yes." Hickman glanced at them all. "I sent the voice recording from the kidnapper to your people at MacKenzie Security. It didn't say anything except that they had her and would be in touch within the next twenty-four hours with a ransom demand."

"I heard it. We all did," Brant said. "Next time we need to demand proof of life."

"Proof of…" Hickman's face paled and it was the first time he'd shown any kind of normal reaction as a father. "They won't get any money if they kill her."

"The fact that they haven't asked for money at this point means that it isn't their reason for the kidnapping," Rush said, his eyes focused on the senator's face for any clue about what was really going on here. His gut told him that this was about Hickman. "So, I have to ask again: who the fuck did you piss off?"

"Rush…" Brant warned but he ignored him.

"I'm going to risk my ass and the lives of all the people who are going to help me get Katrina back in one piece for you. You need to tell me what dirty, rotten things you've been up to and tell me now. I don't mind getting my conscience dirty, you know this, but don't send me out there in the goddam dark."

Hickman stared at him, his eyes shooting daggers and every kind of modern and ancient weaponry he could. Yeah, they hated each other's guts, but that was the same old song on a different fucking day.

"I've recently had to disappoint some of my contacts in the Ukraine."

Rush chewed on that for a minute. "What you mean is that you promised something you can't deliver to some assholes who are the mob or connected to the mob in Eastern Europe."

"My position on the committee for foreign relations requires me to deal with people from more volatile nations. It sometimes happens that they are related to some form of criminal activity. We do our best to navigate the murky waters to achieve security for the United States and our citizens who live abroad."

What a crock of shit.

"And the side deals you make for yourself are just icing on the cake," Rush added.

Hickman glared but he didn't deny it. He knew better than to try and deny it with Rush. He was one of the few men who knew just how many closets full of skeletons this man had. It was why he no longer did any kind of business with him.

"So, just drop the speech and tell me what we need to know to get your daughter back."

Hickman dropped his gaze and sighed. "I have no idea where they could have taken her."

Just before he broke eye contact Rush saw the fear there. One of these people scared him worse than the others, so much that he was hesitant to tell them to save his own daughter.

"Who?"

"The Ukrainians. The Italians. There is a group in Africa I have had dealings with this past month or so."

"Jesus, is there a list?" Brant asked and Rush almost laughed at his tone of incredulity.

"There's *always* a list," Rush offered.

Livvy watched the activity from her perch on the loveseat, her eyes wide with surprise that almost disguised the underlying distaste she obviously had for this entire conversation. Her voice was calm and cool when she spoke.

"Mr. Scott says that you sent us your e-mail and other relevant documents. I'll review them and reach out to my contacts to see if anyone has been approached for alternative, high-end merchandise."

"I'm not sure what that means," Hickman said.

"With the countries you listed and no ransom requested, we have to explore the possibility that Katrina will be offered as a commodity. She's white, young, and sexually inexperienced." The truth was blunt but she delivered it with kindness.

"Oh God," the senator said, his hand shaking a little. "Please don't mention that to my wife…her mother."

"So, you understand how you need to cough up a name. Open up the closet and let all the boogeymen out. We don't have time to fuck around," Rush interjected. He was getting frustrated at this song and dance. "You know that this has to be serious if I'm here at all. I think the last thing I said to you was—"

"I'll see you in hell," Hickman finished.

"Exactly. So don't fuck me around and don't get your daughter killed." Rush advanced on the seated group, uncrossing his arms to point at Hickman. "You know that if anyone can get her out I can, and I'm telling you I will." He pointed at Livvy. "She can find her if you're honest with us."

An older woman with a navy blue suit and a concerned expression entered the room after a brisk knock. "Senator, you have to leave in ten minutes if you're going to the Australian Embassy dinner."

Hickman rose, waving her off. "I think I might cancel…"

"No." Livvy rose to her feet, her hand on his arm. She looked at Brant. They had discussed that she would look for a way to get the senator out of the house so they could have a snoop around. "Shouldn't he keep to his regular schedule?"

Brant stared at her for a moment and then nodded. "Yes. That would be best."

"Fine." He looked at the woman. "Tell them to bring the car around and I'll be down after I change."

"Senator, we'll be in touch," Livvy said, leaning in to brush her cheek against his. Rush watched closely, knowing she was taking the opportunity to return the phone. He only hoped it would tell them what Hickman clearly refused to disclose.

Brant and Livvy filed out and Rush trailed behind them, clenching his hands in fists to resist the urge to grab him and execute enough force on a painful pressure point to force him to tell him what they needed to know.

"Don't be so high and mighty with me, Rush," Hickman snarled under his breath. "I know what you are. I know what you've done."

"I did what my country asked me to do. I should've known better when you were the messenger. I was a grown man and I made my choice to get in bed with the devil. Your daughter is a kid and she can't help who her sperm donor is. My choice is on me." He moved past him but stopped, turning to face the senator. Rush lowered his voice as he leaned in close. "But if Katrina dies because you're a shithead, that's on you."

And then he turned and walked out, promising himself that he would bring the little girl home even if her father didn't deserve her.

Chapter Four

"Atticus, you were right," Olivia said as soon as the door closed on the large, dark SUV.

She watched him in the passenger seat as he stilled and then slowly turned to look at her, a dark eyebrow raised. Her stomach fluttered, a million butterflies. Bloody hell, he was still gorgeous. Actually, he'd been hot before but the hair pushed him over the edge into lush. She wanted to peel off all his clothes, wrap her hand around a hank of his hair, and force him down between her legs.

Damn. Three years and all she'd accomplished was becoming even hotter for the one guy who didn't want her.

"Write that down. I don't think she ever said I was right before, even when we were married." He flashed an unexpected wolfish grin as he glanced at Brant behind the wheel. "Except when she stated that marrying her was the smartest thing I ever did."

"You are an ass," she rebuked him, cutting her eyes to focus outside of the window of the car toward the senator's house. Two story, Georgian townhouse with an ornamental brick wall in the front and a lower wall around the perimeter. She wasn't proficient in DC real estate, but she knew this was a posh neighborhood, full of politicos and the generally rich and well-to-do. This was the United States' equivalent to a peerage and all the earmarks were present—maids answering the door, expensive cars visible in driveways, and security systems.

"Did we get anything off the phone?" she asked, continuing her scan of the house and the line-of-sight from the street.

"Let me call Elena and find out." Brant hit a button on his phone. The ringtone was loud in the vehicle until it ended abruptly when the computer expert picked up. "It's Brant. What did you get from the phone?"

"Nothing really." Her voice sounded dejected over the line and Olivia bit back her groan of frustration in order to listen clearly. "It's practically a burner. A few numbers, no texts. I'm trying to get into his cloud content or his hard drive backup, but we didn't do the cyber security for him. It was set up by a local guy who specializes in server maintenance for politicos. I need a few hours."

Hours they didn't have.

Olivia watched as the metal gate eased back and a black Audi left the property. The windows were blackened sufficiently that she couldn't see anything but shadows. She looked at her watch. Twenty minutes since they'd left.

"Elena, I presume it would be easier if you had the physical hard drive in your possession?" she asked, formulating her plan in her mind.

"Yes, or a download of the data."

"I'm going in to get the hard drive," Oliva said, unfastening her seatbelt and reaching for her purse. She opened it, pulling out the tiny tool kit she'd stashed inside what looked like a cosmetic case and slipping it into the pocket of her shorts. "Brant, what kind of alarm system did you install?"

"Our own design. Wired at the windows, doors, video cameras in every room with motion sensors, external cameras as well."

"You control the monitoring?"

"Yes, but there are people still in the house, so everything will be off except for the door and window contacts. He has round-the-clock security who function as bodyguards and accompany him and his family to events, and there is one always walking the grounds," Brant said.

"Avoiding people is way easier than a set of electronic eyeballs. You alert me to anyone new who enters the house."

"You're not going in there in broad daylight," Atticus growled, shifting to turn full around in his seat to glare at her. "That's insane."

She ignored him. Arguing wouldn't change his mind and she

needed more information. "How many guards in the house and the grounds right now?" Brant flicked a glance between Atticus and her and the low boil of anger in her belly threatened to spill over. "Even when we were married I never promised to obey. You dragged me away from my Mexican paradise to do a job, now let me do it. The last I heard we didn't have time to waste."

Brant sighed, rubbing his face with his palm, the rasp against the stubble loud in the confines of the vehicle. "One guard on the grounds all day. Two inside but he takes one with him when he leaves, so I'm guessing there's only one now. His wife is home and I think he mentioned a nurse with her."

Elena's voice rang out in the car. "Thermal scan shows me a guard on the grounds and three people in the house."

"Thanks, Elena. I owe you a drink," Olivia said.

"Livvy, this is nuts. You can't go in there with no knowledge of the floor plan or the guards' movements," Atticus argued, his tone dark and bossy. His anger was a palpable thing hovering in the air, but there was more and it felt to her like fear.

She scrutinized his face and saw it…he was scared for her. She pushed back the automatic urge to soothe and comfort him. He'd never allowed it when they were married and it wouldn't go over now.

"Does anyone is this car think he's going to tell us anything useful? Does anyone else think he'd let his daughter die or worse to save his ass?" She looked at both of the men, daring them to contradict her. "I'm not debating this. I've gone in on jobs with less time and information. I'm going." She popped in the earbud he had given her earlier. "You can monitor my movements and alert me to any changes."

"Fuck!" Atticus practically shouting and quickly undoing his seatbelt was the last thing she heard as she darted from the SUV and crossed the street, one dwelling down from the Hickman house. She blended into the falling shadows of the wall, scanning the neighborhood to see if anyone was actually out on the street. Nobody. Good.

"Are you going to break in to their house wearing those goddam heels?" Atticus asked, his voice beyond frustrated in her ear.

"I can do all kinds of things in these heels. You know this," she teased, inching down to a place where the brick wall sloped down to half the original height. She hiked her leg over and slid down onto the ground.

"I totally see why you married her," Brant said in her ear.

Atticus's reply was a dark and broody "Shut up."

She ignored them both and scanned the twilight-infused area. "Can you give me an idea of where the outdoor guard is located?"

Silence passed for a few moments and then Elena's voice joined the others in her head. "Heat scan shows that he's in the northwest corner. Near the garage."

The opposite place from where she was now. She could work with that.

"Excellent, I'll go through the sunroom."

"I just deactivated the alarm," Elena said. "No alarms will sound when you open an external door or window. I can't turn off anything that we didn't create and install, so keep an eye out for random security measures."

"Thanks, Elena." She took a deep breath and steadied her hands. They were shaking with the adrenaline from her excitement. She loved this, loved getting into places she didn't belong.

Olivia bolted across the lawn, sliding into the gloom as soon as she could. The sunroom door was easy, the lock in the doorknob and the deadbolt giving way under the skill of her fingers and tools. She slipped inside and shut the door quietly behind her, standing perfectly still as she listened for sounds of the staff.

Footsteps above, directly overhead. The rush of water and then the steps again, crossing the room.

"Is the master bedroom on the back of the house?" she whispered, hoping they could still hear her.

"Yes. Across the entire back above where you are," Elena answered. "The private office is the second door on the right as you exit the sunroom."

"Thanks." Olivia crept across the room, keeping to the edges as much as she could until she got to the door. Another pause as she listened. Footsteps overhead. Nothing on this floor that she could hear. "Better now than never."

Swift, sure movement down the hall. One door. Stopping at

the second and pausing to press her ear against the heavy wood. Nothing that she could hear from the office but Atticus almost made her jump.

"What the fuck is going on in there? Livvy, talk to me."

She bit her lip and focused on easing the door open and getting her ass out of the hallway where anyone could find her. She shut the door behind her and quickly scanned the room before answering him.

"Atticus, please shut up. I'm trying to work and your squawking in my ear is not bloody helping."

"I'm not trying to help. You need to get your sweet ass out of there."

"This is not the time for you and I to discuss how sweet my ass is. Just shut up and let me steal a hard drive and get out of here."

"Livvy," he said, his belligerent tone grating on every last nerve she had.

"I'm taking out my earbud," she said and pried the small piece out of her ear and put it in her pocket. The silence was a beautiful thing. Now, to get down to business.

She walked over to the spotless desk and groaned. All-in-one monitors and CPUs were a bitch to carry.

"Come on, where's your backup?" It had to be smaller, easier to carry and conceal just in case she got caught leaving the house.

She kneeled down, pulling open drawers and doors on the large wooden desk. So many of them were locked but one slid open, a panel covering a deep, ventilated space. Wires fed through the side and there, sitting in the middle on a cradle-type stand, was a hard drive. As big as a hardcover book, it would be easy to move.

"Bingo." She laughed softly, pulled the cables and wires from the back of it and removed it from the space and carefully closed the door. She fished into her pocket and popped the earbud back in. "I've got it and I'm heading out."

"Goddam it, Livvy," Atticus's voice immediately filled the space, tinged with enough worry to make her feel a little guilty. Just a little bit. "Get the hell out of there. Hickman came back."

She froze. That wasn't what she'd expected to hear.

"Oh fuck," she breathed out, making her way across the room and stopping to listen at the door. Brant had joined Atticus in her ear with his insistence that she get out of the house as soon as possible. Her heart was pounding and it was hard enough to concentrate without their noise. "I can't think with you two in my head. I'll see you outside."

Popping the earbud out for the second time, she leaned against the cool wood of the door and listened for movement in the hallway. Running through the layout in her mind, she recalled a large center hallway, a center staircase dissecting the first floor with formal rooms to the left and right. She'd glimpsed a kitchen straight ahead in the back, past the office, with a known exit through the sunroom or the front door.

Male voices were loud in the entranceway, growing louder as they approached the door she was currently hugging.

"Bugger." Olivia turned, looking around the room for possible hiding places. Everything was open and too small to hide a grown woman. Except the couch. Maybe she could bend down behind it? "I can't believe I have to roll around on the floor in $400 Dolce shorts."

It was better than being caught red-handed, and she'd send the dry cleaning bill to Atticus, so she launched herself across the room and flung herself behind the back of the sofa just as the door opened. Olivia curled up as tightly as she could with a hard drive stuck to her chest and held her breath.

Hickman entered the room, his security guard trailing behind him. He tossed his tuxedo jacket on the chair next to the couch, walked to his desk and sat down behind the computer. Biting back the "oh fuck" that almost erupted from between her lips, she hunched even lower, praying for the power of invisibility. Hickman was rattling on about hating to leave the dinner early, but she didn't care what he was saying, unless he began emoting about his intention to leave this office and let her get the hell out.

A woman dressed in a scrub top, polyester pants, and sensible shoes appeared at the door. "Senator Hickman, your wife is awake and asking for you."

"I'll be right there," he answered, rising from his chair and heading for the door. "Stewart, please let me know the status once you make your rounds."

"Yes, sir. I'll check in with Alex on the grounds and give you a full report. We have two extra men on duty tonight and in the future until Miss Hickman is returned and the threat is eliminated."

They both left the room, the senator heading up the stairs and the very capable Stewart making a right and moving toward the kitchen. Olivia scrambled as quickly as she could in three-inch heels and soft-shoed toward the door. A stop at the door, just long enough to glance left, right, and up the stairs, and she bolted across the black and white marble of the of the entryway, flipped the locks on the large, black door, and opened it.

The twilight had turned into night and she slowed her roll as she stepped out onto the large, marble step. Acting as if she had every right to be there, Olivia closed the door behind her and casually made her way to the sidewalk and then across the street to where the dark SUV was waiting. The front passenger door opened just as she reached out to open her own and Atticus leapt out and grabbed her by the shoulders.

His fingers bit into the flesh there but it was the fear that edged his voice that made her wince. Everything about him was raw and exposed, from the wild look in his dark eyes to the hard set of his jaw and the slight tremble in his fingers.

"What the fuck were you thinking?" he asked, his gaze daring her to be anything but honest.

"I was doing my job, Atticus. The one you brought me here to accomplish." She reached out the hand that wasn't holding the hard drive and touched his cheek, watching as he shut his eyes and leaned toward her. Their foreheads touched and he rocked against her, a low growl of frustration rumbling in the space between them. "You've got to stop treating me like fine china."

"But you're so fucking breakable," he said, leaning in to press a hard kiss to her mouth. It was brief, just a clash of teeth and tangle of tongues. Enough to leave them both panting when it was over. "You're going to kill me, Livvy. So help me God, you will."

Atticus opened her door and half shoved, half assisted her into the backseat. The door slammed behind her and she watched silently as he hauled his large body into the passenger seat and took his obvious frustrations out on his door. For her part, she concentrated on putting her tools back in her bag and thinking about anything but how that kiss ignited a hunger in her belly that threatened to claw its way out.

The fact that there was an answering need emanating from Atticus toward her was only a small comfort. Nobody wanted to be in this place alone, especially when she was completely on her own in anything beyond the physical.

She refused to acknowledge the twist and throb a little higher and just under her rib cage. Olivia knew that her emotional and physical reactions to Atticus were so intertwined that it was impossible to separate them, but she'd never let him know. Things had begun with them as a strictly sexual thing and she could keep it on that level if that's what it took to make it through this job. He didn't feel the same way about her and she'd come to terms with that long ago.

"Did you just walk out the front door? Just like you belonged there?" Brant asked her as he turned around, his tone incredulous. When she grinned, he laughed. "You've got balls, Lady Olivia."

Atticus sighed heavily. "Don't fucking encourage her."

She clicked on her seatbelt, calming her heart rate as they pulled away from the curb and headed to Atticus's house. She couldn't help but smile with satisfaction at completing her task. There was no denying how much she loved it.

"Sometimes the most obvious choice is the right one."

Chapter Five

"Come on, Rush, admit it. You're Batman."

Elena teased him from the table in the large, upstairs loft space he used as his DC base. From the outside it looked practically abandoned, with graffiti and bars over the windows. It didn't encourage Girl Scouts selling cookies or anyone else with any sense. He owned the entire building, situated in a so-so area of the district, and used the downstairs open space to keep a motorcycle, a truck, and his own gym. A large, open patio extended out from the second floor living area with a view of the Capital and the Washington Monument in the distance. This was a pretty town if you ignored all the dirt and sleaze.

He missed his cabin in Montana and his dogs.

"I'm not Batman. He's a sociopath. I'm just a dick," he answered, taking a bite of pizza and a swig from his beer. He'd only allow himself one since he had no idea when he'd have to suit up and go get Katrina, but he needed something to calm him down after that stunt Livvy had pulled at Hickman's house.

He'd sat mute in the truck, the feeling of helplessness making him grind his teeth together with his effort not to throw back his head and howl. It had been his nightmare scenario: Livvy in danger and him powerless to stop it or protect her. It was the fact that she willingly sought out the risk that made him nuts. When he'd discovered who she was and what she did it was fear that had made him lash out and threaten to turn her in. Absolute. Fucking. Terror.

And by the time he'd gotten a grip on what he felt, she was

gone and it was too late to change anything between them.

She sat on one of the long, leather sofas right now—furniture she'd chosen when they were married—eating and laughing with Brant and completely at ease. He watched her until her gaze clashed with his own and there was no mistaking the flare of heat in her eyes. Livvy's cheeks flushed with her reaction to him and he wanted to take her into his room and fuck her on his king-sized bed until she screamed his name and the cops showed up because the neighbors called it in.

Then, when they'd left he'd take her again. Slow and sweet, coaxing her pleasure out of her until she melted against him and begged for more in the quiet, breathy way he loved.

Breakable. Precious. The most gorgeous thing he'd ever been able to call his own and she risked her life as if it meant nothing. It still made him nuts.

Elena interrupted his thoughts as she continued to clack away at her computer, which was hooked up to the stolen hard drive. "Whatever. I dig your Batcave and its crazy fast WiFi connection." She hit a couple more keys and raised her fists in triumph. "Especially when I get these results."

Everyone in the room scrambled to get in close to hear what she'd found. They'd heard nada from the kidnappers for the past couple of hours and it was making him twitchy to sit around and do nothing. He wasn't built that way.

"I was able to hack into Hickman's financials and e-mails from what I pulled from the hard drive." She smiled at Olivia and winked her thank you. Livvy nodded her head in acknowledgement. "He's definitely dealing with a lot of assholes, but one in particular dumped a lot of money into an offshore account for Hickman right before e-mails started flying back and forth in a fast, furious, and then increasingly hostile manner."

"Let me guess. Hickman took the money and failed to deliver." Rush made the not-so-hard leap of logic.

Elena waved a hand at the pizza boxes on the island. "Hand that man another slice of pepperoni."

"Just give me the name of the animal who took Katrina and keep the damn pizza," Rush ground out, his fingers digging into the back of the chair in front of him. "Seriously, I'm all out of patience right now."

"Umbuerto Figueroa," Elena answered as silence fell around the table. "The Butcher of Buenaventura."

"Jesus," Rush said on an exhale and it was a prayer. The best he could do for a little girl with big freckles and a talent for drawing pictures of dogs of every breed. He still had those drawings, every single one, with a couple framed and hanging in the cabin. Katrina had been his only constant pen pal when he was deployed, except for Livvy, and she would always be special to him.

His stomach twisted up so tightly that he gasped and grabbed his side. He was afraid he would be sick at the thought of what that evil motherfucker would do to Katrina if he didn't get his way.

"Drugs, prostitutes, children, organs, art...you name it and he exploits it for his own gain," Rush murmured. "He kidnaps and murders, has his own militia. Hickman is in way over his head and his daughter is in the hands of a man who doesn't care who he hurts."

The slide of a warm, soft hand into his own brought him up short and he turned his head to find Livvy there beside him. She didn't touch him anywhere else but he felt it down in his marrow. Her gray eyes were clear with her trust in him, her conviction that he had this. It didn't make his anger and rage go away but it helped him to focus, helped him to see beyond his desire to run off half-cocked with no set plan.

"He wouldn't take her out of the country, would he?" Brant said, thinking out loud. He shook his head. "No. Not yet. He'd have her nearby until he gave his demands to Hickman."

"She'll be with his local hands and feet. He's not going to be anywhere near this just in case it goes badly. Plausible deniability is his Teflon coating. Nothing sticks to him," Rush added, dipping his head and thinking hard about his knowledge of Figueroa's known contacts. It *would be* someone local. Not a thug or a street kid but someone well connected who had no problem dipping his whole foot into something disgusting. His head snapped up and he locked eyes with Elena. "Does Hickman have any contact with a guy named Paulo Guzzi?"

Elena dropped her focus back to the screen, her fingers flying over the keys as she searched for the information. Rush knew the answer before she said it because her expression morphed into one of predatory glee.

"Yes. All the time."

"So, we just have to find and *gently* persuade this Guzzi guy to cough up the whereabouts of Katrina," Brant said, his grin almost feral. "Elena, start a search and figure out where we can find him."

Rush's eyes snapped to Livvy as understanding passed between them. A smile tugged at her lips and a devilish light danced in her eyes before she turned to the people gathered around the table.

"I know how to get him to come to us," she said at the same time he started shaking his head.

"No. This is where you get off this crazy train, Livvy."

She ignored him, taking her phone out of her pocket and scrolling through her contacts. "Atticus Rush, you couldn't boss me around when we were married, I don't know why you think you can now. I'm calling Carla and getting the ball rolling, so just calm your ass down." He opened his mouth to protest when she smiled and began speaking with the woman who'd answered the call. "Carla, it's Olivia. I'm in town and I need a bit of a favor." She smiled and laughed, her eyes sliding to the right and twinkling just a little. "You name the Prada bag and Atticus will get it for you."

He watched her, straining to hear the other side of the conversation but unable to pick up anything but the briefest pieces of it. He was very aware of the curious looks he was getting from the rest of the team but ignored them. He didn't know them well and they'd obviously known very little about his marriage and nothing about the woman who'd taken his name. He was a private man so he was sure they were eating up any crumb, and he had the uneasy feeling that they'd know even more before this mission was done.

"I'm helping Atticus and his friends find a kidnapped girl and we really need to talk to Paulo Guzzi, so I was wondering if he's at Club D tonight. Sure, I can wait until you check." Time clicked by in anxious silence but Carla was quick because within seconds Livvy's mouth broke into a huge grin. "Can you make sure he knows I'll be there tonight? Don't mention anything about Atticus. Call me back and let me know. Thanks."

She ended the call and looked around triumphantly. Atticus

wanted to throttle her.

"What is Club D and why would Paulo want to know you are there?" Brant asked, his expression confused.

"It's a private club and he's always been interested in me," Livvy answered, her words careful but not with embarrassment. No, she was never one to carry shame over any choice she made. Her discretion was all for him, her eyes asking what she could divulge to the people in the room.

He didn't care who knew about his preferences but this was not the time or the place to discuss his kink.

"Interested in you..." Elena let her voice trail off as the meaning became clear. "Oh. *Interested*."

"We met Paulo a few years ago at Club D and he always made his interest known, but we steered clear of him. It's no secret that he's a scumbag." Rush directed a glare at Livvy. "Which is why we shouldn't be baiting him with something he cannot have."

"We need to grab him as soon as we can, right? This is the best way to ensure he will be at a certain place at a certain time, and definitely not expecting an ambush with very little or no security," Livvy concluded in a tone that made his teeth grind together. She was so cavalier to throw herself into danger.

It pissed him off and scared the shit out of him but he couldn't argue that it wasn't a good plan. He also couldn't just stand here and wait for Carla Ambroghetti to call back. He'd lose his mind. He stomped across the room and headed for the stairs.

"I'm going to work out before I do something stupid like agree with this plan."

Chapter Six

"Was he like this when you were married?" Brant asked.

Olivia watched him stomp out of the kitchen and head down the stairs to the first floor of the building. His broad back was rigid, fists clenching at his sides. Atticus was pissed. It was probably best to give him his space...for now.

"Oh yes. What you see with Atticus is what you get, although it isn't always what you want."

He chuckled under his breath, nodding his head toward the large leather sofa to sit down. They settled next to each other and she knew an interrogation disguised as a friendly talk was coming. She was a largely unknown quantity to this man except for her reputation as a thief, and that knowledge was courtesy of Atticus. It was a testament to what good friends they were that Brant brought her on this team with nothing more than her ex-husband's recommendation.

She wondered if he would dive right in or take a more circuitous route to what he wanted to know. She guessed a dive off the high board but wasn't sure. He didn't disappoint.

"So, why did you two break up?"

Olivia raised an eyebrow at him. "I think you know why."

"The stealing of things that don't belong to you?"

"And I didn't even have to give you a clue." They both laughed but when they settled down she continued in a more serious tone. Losing the only man she'd ever loved really wasn't a laughing matter. "I think it was the fact I lied to him about it for so long, at least by omission. Either way, Atticus was pretty black and white with his morality back then. Maybe now too. I can't pretend to know him all that well anymore, if I ever did."

"I think you know him better than most."

She thought about it, watching Elena work steadily at the computer for a few minutes before answering. "We're not that different, all outward appearances aside."

"Really? An earl's daughter and an orphan kid from Baltimore?"

She wasn't going to share Atticus's backstory. It wasn't hers to tell.

"I don't really have a sob story. I'm the youngest child and the only daughter of my father. My mother was his second wife and instead of May-December it was more of a January-December romance. I barely got to know him before he passed away and my brother took the title. I spent most of my life in boarding schools but so did most of the girls in my position. My mother moved in and out of my life as her opulent lifestyle allowed and my brothers were all so much older that we had very little in common."

This is where she and Atticus were so much alike, and no one would ever guess without having their history. They'd been cared for by people who'd been paid to care and that made you view relationships differently. His life in the foster system and hers in impersonal, expensive boarding schools surrounded them with people who gave them what they needed but never *needed* them. It hadn't taken her long to realize that it was what drew them together. The desire to be needed by at least one other person.

But she'd been the only one to give in to that deep desire. It had kept her in love with him all this time while he'd let her go and moved on.

Brant interrupted her mind drift.

"So you learned to steal because…?" He drew the question out and barely left room for her to answer before he filled in his own answers. "To get attention? To piss your family off?"

She waved off his guesses with a derisive scoff. "I did it to get the answers to exams for me and my friends or to get extra sweets. I realized I was good at it and then started pilfering things at some of my mother's parties, and when I didn't get caught I became braver. I studied lock-picking and safe-cracking, and learned so much on the job and from a pair of French thieves who were willing to train and share their knowledge. I loved it and I still do. It's exhilarating."

The only thing that had ever come close was being with Atticus.

"Except for the stealing from innocent people part," Brant said, his judgment showing. She wasn't surprised but she also didn't buy into it and never had.

"I don't really do that anymore. Don't tell anyone but I've been more into the business of reuniting rightful owners with their lost valuables lately. I do it for a small fee since I don't really need the money." Olivia laughed at his shocked expression. "Oh, don't look like that. I occasionally procure a bauble or something for myself. Something glittery and rare. I'm not *completely* reformed."

He considered for a moment, his fingers tapping on the arm of the sofa. Olivia let him stew, mildly curious about what he could be hesitating to ask her. Probably something about Club D or Atticus. When he finally spoke, it wasn't at all what she expected.

"I could use someone with your skills at MacKenzie."

"What?" It sounded like he was offering her a job but that was ludicrous. "I don't think I'm cut out for an office job, Brant. I was not born to punch a clock."

He shook his head, his smile devilish and his body leaning forward, all indicators that he thought this was a great idea.

"This wouldn't be nine-to-five. I could use you to test security systems, help design ones for tricky facilities. Who better to keep thieves from breaking in than a world-class thief? You could be a consultant."

"I don't know," she said, shifting uncomfortably in her seat. It wasn't that she hated the idea but the fact that she wasn't outright turning him down that made her squirm. Did it appeal to her? Maybe it did. "I'd have to think about it."

Brant opened his mouth to say something but the ringing of her phone interrupted their conversation. She looked down on the screen and saw Carla's name on the display. She flashed it at Brant, who nodded when she took the call.

She listened to her friend on the line and smiled, glad that another part of this puzzle was coming together. When she clicked off with a "thank you," she rose from her seat.

"Paulo will be at Club D in two hours. Carla told him that I will be there and hinted that I'll be there to play. She'll arrange a private room for us and we can grab him."

"That's almost too easy," Brant said.

"It will be up to you and Atticus to get any information out of him and if that fails, I can look over his place and see if there is any indication that he orchestrated the kidnapping."

"I think it's a solid plan but Rush will be pissed."

"I'll tell him. I need to work out and he can yell at me and get over it before we have to leave."

"So you think you can soothe the savage beast?"

Olivia shook her head. "There's no soothing Atticus. You just let him roar and get it out of his system."

Chapter Seven

Pushing his body to the limit was still the best way to get out of his head.

In Baltimore as a kid in foster care and group homes, he'd found solace in the gym at the local YMCA. The activities varied depending on funding and volunteers, but there was always some random stash of equipment and he would spend hours learning to use it. Building his body, developing strength and endurance was essential for a boy with no one in the world to have his back.

He'd never known his parents, never had any family. Hell, his own name had been chosen by a caseworker, a combination of the name of a character from her favorite book and a randomly selected name out of the phone book.

His strength and discipline had gotten him through BUDS training and the years of deployment and nightmare-inducing missions. Pushing his body had given him a place to shove his rage. It was therapy via barbell and boxing ring. Without the outlet he'd have lost his mind, lashed out at the world or eaten his gun.

The only thing that had ever had the same effect was Livvy. Her arms around him had soothed the monsters lurking in the dark recesses of his mind.

But she could also piss him off faster than anything or anyone.

She was his savior and his sin.

So it didn't help when she followed him into his gym space, wearing nothing but an athletic bra and tiny boy shorts. She ignored his glare, only giving him a quick glance and a flash of white teeth in a half smile. She looked like the damn Cheshire cat, and it wouldn't have surprised him to see a furry tail swishing in the air in triumph. She knew he was pissed and her favorite game was "how far can I push Rush?"

It was best to ignore her. She had other ideas.

"I need to stretch before we head over to Club D. Carla called and we're on for later. The stress has my body in knots. Is this okay?"

What could he say and not sound like an ass?

"There are a couple of mats over there if you need them." He nodded toward the corner of the gym area. "Help yourself."

He added two more weights and inserted the pins in the slots before centering himself, planting his feet in the correct stance and squatting in front of the metal bar. He took a deep breath, gripped the rod and gritted his teeth, lifting from a core of strength he had buried down deep.

Once in a standing position, he executed three perfect lifts over his head before lowering the bar to the floor with a giant exhale and a rattle of metal. He stood and glanced over to Livvy, so glad he'd waited until the weights were on the floor before he did it.

She was executing her yoga moves with a sexy, sensual grace that hardened his cock in his thin shorts. She was…bendy…extremely limber. An expert gymnast, it was a skill set that helped her get in and out of tight and unusual places. It was also something he'd thoroughly enjoyed when she'd been wrapped around him and he was buried deep inside her. Damn. He adjusted his hard-on and turned to the pull-up bars mounted overhead.

Something else that working out was good for—dealing with inappropriate boners for your ex-wife.

He shook out chalk on his hands, dusted off the excess and leapt to the lowest bar, beginning the first of many pull-ups. His muscles burned in the best way, his mind easing off the ledge of anger and fear he'd had in his gut since Brant had showed up on his doorstep. Yeah, he was worried for Katrina, but now he had Livvy in the mix and her little show today had shaved at least a year off his life.

She'd been the first person he'd ever worried about, had ever been afraid he would lose. As a foster kid he'd never been close enough to anyone to care. People moved in and out, there one day and gone the next. He didn't worry about the guys in his unit. They were trained professionals and knew how to take care of themselves. The possibility of final, deathly circumstances had been part of what they'd signed up for when they'd put on the uniform, and while you never wanted to lose a brother-in-arms, it happened. You couldn't do the job if you were worried about bad shit happening.

But Livvy…she'd risked her neck for nothing and it made him nuts.

He gritted his teeth and pulled his body up and as far over the bar as he could, lowering himself and then doing it again. Sweat ran down his face and his bare chest but he ignored it.

A shift in the air next to him broke his concentration and he opened his eyes and looked over. Livvy was next to him, her hands wrapped around the bar, sculpted muscles in her arms and back moving under her soft skin with each lift of her body. She was strong and sexy and he groaned with the clench of lust in his gut.

He paused his own movements, watching her as she executed her moves with precise control. A bead of sweat rolled down from her temple, disappearing into the soft hair pulled loose from her ponytail, and he licked his lips with the desire to follow its path and taste her.

"Bloody hell," she panted, hanging suspended from the bar, her chest heaving with her exertion. She locked eyes with him, her words stuttering as she struggled for breath. "I'm out of shape."

He scoffed and he spoke in spite of the lust choking him. "Not even close. Your body is still amazing."

"Nobody works me out like you used to, Atticus. You're a brutal taskmaster."

"You were an easy student." She had been a great workout partner, never afraid to try something new or to push her body to its limits. It was the thing that had attracted him to her the first night they'd met. Livvy enjoyed the physical, was open to push her boundaries every chance she got. She could meet him step for step, limit for limit.

Her gray eyes darkened and he knew she was remembering the same thing. He glanced down and her hard nipples were visible through the thin spandex of her top, his eyes torn away from the gorgeous sight by her movement toward him.

"What are you doing?" he asked but he knew, his hands tightening his grip on the bar when she wrapped her legs around his waist and looped her arms around his neck. He groaned, not just with the added weight but with the full, searing contact of their bodies.

They'd done this a million times before. Instead of him adding weights to his legs to increase the impact, Livvy had served as his extra measure. Ending up on the floor in a tangle of mouths and limbs was the usual result and his favorite way to end the workout.

"Working out," she grinned, the challenge in her eyes almost blotting out the desire. Almost. "Today was stressful for both of us. I think we have some tension we need to work off."

"Some 'good guy' lecture I got from Brant told me that I should say this is a bad idea."

"Ah, but you always love the bad idea."

"I do."

"So, let's be bad."

He groaned, his muscles screaming with the strain of holding them both up and the sexual tension sticking them together like a magnet and steel. Rush gritted his teeth and glared. But he didn't say no. There wasn't enough willpower in the world to get him to do that.

"How many reps do you want to do?" she asked, her words coming out in panting breaths against his lips. The same words she'd said so many times before, the same woman. It was the best fucking déjà vu he'd ever had.

"Twenty." He leaned his forehead against hers, eyes locked in challenge, encouragement, and lust. He adjusted his body against hers and his full, hard cock slid right in between the sweet "v" of her thighs. He groaned and she gasped.

You could fake the intensity of sex with hookers and people who didn't get under your skin. Getting off was easy, but chemistry was impossible to fake and they had it. They were as dangerously combustible as homemade explosives, and he realized that this moment had been inevitable. Their highly matched sexual compatibly was the one part that always worked. This was how they relieved stress, both physically wired with their release valve tied directly to sex.

It didn't have to be anything else. They could let off some steam and let it be nothing but a little bit of fun between consenting adults.

Livvy lowered a hand from around his neck and trailed it over his chest and around his waist. The sharp slap of her palm against his ass made them both jump. He shifted his grip on the bar.

"Get to it, Atticus. Give me twenty," she challenged, her eyes promising a reward if he was a good boy.

He exhaled and pulled them up until both of their chins cleared the bar, and then he slowly lowered them down. Livvy's hand slipped inside the waistband of his shorts, her palm sliding down his ass cheek, stopping only to give him a squeeze.

"One," she said, her lips barely touching his own.

He lifted them both again, his muscles straining with the effort.

"Two," she counted, the briefest swipe of her tongue along his lower lip pushing him into another rep.

Rush powered through the rest of the pull-ups, his body screaming with the physical effort and his cock hard as steel against the heat of her core. Sweat slicked them both, Livvy's muscles straining with her effort to hang on until he'd completed the last one.

"Twenty," she mumbled around his tongue's invasion into her mouth. She tasted like heat and spice and the coppery hint of blood from biting into her lower lip. Rush released his grip on the bar and they both fell. He maintained enough balance with her wrapped around him to adjust quickly and lower them to the mat in a controlled plummet.

Rush spread his body out over hers, grabbing her hands and lifting them over her head to pin them to the mat as he kissed her. Ate at her with his lips and tongue and teeth. Livvy kept her legs wrapped around his waist, grinding up as he thrust against her. He could come just like this. Sweaty and clothed and horny as a teenager.

He released her mouth, looking down to find her eyes wide open, pupils blown dark with her need. She bit into her bottom lip, her fingernails digging into the flesh of his hands in an echo of her frustration.

"You want to do this?" he asked, giving her an out if she also realized what a bad idea this really was. "I want to make you come, I want to come all over you, but I can go jerk off in the shower if this isn't what you want."

"We started out playing around." She shook her head, leaning up to kiss him lightly. "We do sex, strictly physical sex, very well. That's all I'm looking for right now."

Her "right now" didn't escape his notice, and a part of him was dying to ask if there could ever be more than "right now" ever again, but he didn't. He scanned her face, gauging whether she was being straight with him. They'd never had a problem with honesty and sex. Just honesty and everything else.

"Come on, Atticus, drop and give me another twenty."

He raised an eyebrow at that one.

"Okay, give me just one. A *really good* one."

He smiled at that one. "You are a fucking pain in my ass, Lady Livvy. You make me nuts."

She bucked up her hips and he closed his eyes, grinding his dick into her.

"Fine. Work out your issues on me and I'll use you so that this is mutually cheap and superficial." She struggled under him, her legs opening wider. "Now."

"Goddam you…" He looked down at her, hair loose from her ponytail and spread out in an angle. Arms raised over her head and breasts thrust upward. He swallowed hard, biting back all the things he'd say if he ever had the words. He wasn't a words guy so he got back to what he did best. "…just goddam."

He dipped his head, taking her mouth in a deep, rough kiss. He didn't have it in him to be gentle right now. Three years and a heart-stopping afternoon of Livvy risking her neck and he was all need and want and aggression.

Rush released her hands, finding the zipper of her athletic bra in between her breasts and lowering it. The fabric sprang back, her nipples hardening into tighter buds when exposed to the air. He licked the droplet of sweat off her skin and then sucked a hard peak into his mouth.

Livvy cried out, her back bowing off the mat, her fingernails digging into his shoulder with enough force to make him wince. His dick got even harder with the thought of his back marred with her stripes.

He kissed down her chest, scraping her pale skin with his teeth, creating his own pattern on her body. Rush eased his body lower, pressing her thighs open with his shoulders as he dipped his fingers into the crotch of her shorts, tugging them to the side to give him access to the place he most wanted to be.

"Fuck, you're so slick," he growled, dragging his finger across her pussy, spreading around her lube. He slid a finger inside her, burying his face against her stomach and biting down with the sensation of sliding into her tight, wet heat. He dragged his lips down, across the spandex of her clothing until he found her clit. "I want you to come hard. On my tongue. I want to taste it, Livvy."

She lifted her head, caught his gaze, and wove her fingers into his hair. She yanked on it, the sting on his scalp only heightening his desire and forcing out a tight laugh.

"Do it. Come on."

Her wish had always been his command, and this time was no different. The first shock of her flavor on his tongue made him shiver. The second made him shift on his knees, giving his cock more room in his shorts. It didn't ease the ache in his balls so he used his one free hand to shove his shorts down in the front, enough to free his dick and wrap his hand around it.

"Sweet pussy," he murmured against her flesh, dragging his teeth lightly over her swollen lips. "So fucking delicious." *And mine.* He lowered his head and covered her again in his only hope to not voice that bat-shit-crazy thought.

He pumped two fingers in and out of her body, lapping and swirling at her clit with firm strokes and speeding up as her moans grew louder and louder. Livvy writhed under him, her heels digging into the mat with force as she pressed against his mouth in a greedy, wordless plea.

"Right there." Her voice was low, vibrating along his skin. "Right. Fucking. There."

She went off like a bottle rocket, her body lifting up as she rocked up onto her toes. He groaned, dissolving into light laughter when she grabbed his ears and kept his mouth on her as she rode out the last of the pleasure ripping through her body.

"God save the Queen," she muttered and he let the sharp laugh escape. He'd forgotten that she said that after she came. When he'd asked, she said it was when she most grateful to be a free, modern female citizen of the United Kingdom. It was just natural to be patriotic.

He settled back on his heels, looking down her while he stroked his dick. Livvy was lying back on the mat, bare breasts heaving with each breath as she flung her arms open wide. Her eyes were bright, cheeks flushed deep pink, streaks of beard burn on her skin. She looked edible and so very fuckable.

"Come on and get inside me," she said, as if she could read his mind.

He dropped his head, shaking it with the realization that he was wholly unprepared for this moment. It was stupid, considering how Livvy and he always were around each other. It was a miracle if they could keep their clothes on in public.

"I don't have a condom down here," he said.

She stared at him, letting the news soak in. "There's more than one way for me to get you off."

She drifted her fingertips down his chest and abdomen, snagging them in the waistband of his shorts, caressing the swollen head that protruded above the fabric. His body bucked forward and he moaned, brushing aside her hand to reach in and stroke himself.

"I want your mouth," he growled.

Chapter Eight

Good. She wanted to taste him.

Olivia licked her lips, watching him as he moved up her body until he straddled her chest. Atticus stroked his cock, shoving his shorts down to his thighs with his free hand, baring almost his entire gorgeous body to her. His eyes never left her face and she could feel the singe of his gaze on her skin.

He made her hot and achy, the fever of lust causing her to squirm as she felt her own arousal bouncing back from its temporary respite granted by her orgasm. She never fooled herself that one was enough or would satisfy her hunger for him. It had burrowed in deep from their first night together and once she'd fallen in love? It was a living, breathing animal that she'd been unable to contain.

"Come closer." Olivia reached out and wrapped her fingers around the wide girth of his dick, joining his own slow strokes up and down the shaft. She dragged her gaze from his to their movement, lifting up to lick the pre-cum pearling on the tip.

She moaned at the salty sweet taste of him and he gasped, his entire body tensing for a moment before relaxing enough to give her control. Olivia slipped a hand around his ass cheek and nudged him closer, encouraging him to thrust as she licked him up and down, lingering over the vein bulging just under the flushed skin, knowing it would only make him harder.

"I want to fuck your mouth," he half requested/half demanded as he dropped his grip on his cock and traced the tip of it over her lips.

She shivered, loving how he wanted her. It was primal and dirty and real.

"I wish we had time to play at Club D," she whispered as she cupped his balls and caressed the sack with her mouth and fingers.

He jerked and growled a little bit, a rumbling she felt deep in her own sex as she squirmed under him. Damn, she was getting close again. Just the feel of him on her lips, the taste on her tongue, his dark, earthy scent surrounding her.

"Fuck yes," he agreed, taking himself in hand to press inside her lips, slowly and a little bit at a time. She wasn't sure if he was teasing himself or her, but it worked. "I'd take you in front of everyone, letting them watch as you came apart under me. I'd find a third, maybe Carla, loving the view as I worked myself in and out of your pussy."

He thrust into her mouth as his words spun around them in the heated, humid air of the gym. Olivia relaxed, trusting him as she had so many times before to always push her to the edge of her comfort zone but never beyond. Her lips were wrapped around his cock and she loved the stretch due to his size, the heft of him on her tongue.

She reached down between her legs and stroked her own aching flesh in time with his movements. She was so close, so achingly close to another orgasm that her eyes fluttered shut at the first touch.

"Open your eyes and look at me, Livvy." It was a common demand of his, wanting that connection between them. Sometimes she needed it too and sometimes it was too much, forcing her into a headspace she wasn't always thrilled to be in. That place forced her to face her true feelings and the knowledge that he didn't feel the same way.

His gaze was brutally dark, filled with all of the hard things that made him who he was. Pain and cynicism warred with the edges of tenderness and the fire of his desire. She saw everything he was in that moment—a man who'd been hardened by life but would accept kindness and affection from only a few. Not because he wanted to be cruel but because he didn't trust it.

But it was also clear that he wanted her. He cared deeply for her. But there was no love on his part.

Atticus wasn't built that way.

"You need to come again?" he asked, snapping her back to the present as his thrusts into her mouth sped up. "Are you touching that sweet pussy? Wishing it was my tongue, my lips? Slide your fingers inside and pretend it's me fucking you, baby."

She moaned, letting her eyes slide shut this time and keeping them that way. She planted her feet on the ground, bending her knees as she slid two fingers inside her, plunging in and out in time with his own hard pace.

"Come on, Livvy." His finger glided along her cheekbone and she opened her eyes, watching the sweat roll down his face and naked chest, taking in the strain in his muscles as he fucked her. "I'm so close, baby. Come one more time and I'll blow, I swear."

It was too much. Atticus taking her mouth and her own hand finding all the places that would get her off fast. The orgasm was hard enough to bow her back off the mat and she writhed underneath the small part of his weight she did carry as he straddled her. His thighs were trembling with his effort not to crush her and to hold off his own pleasure until she came again.

Atticus let out a jumble of wordless encouragement as he leaned forward, the perfect angle to thrust his cock into her mouth with sexy sharp snaps of his hips. His forearm muscles bulged as he braced himself on each side of her head. Olivia ran both of her hands up his thighs, cupped his ass cheeks, and delved between the taut muscles. With fingers slick with her own lube she found his hole and circled once before sliding inside with the perfect pressure against the tight ring of muscle.

"Holy shit, yes," he groaned over her and thrust a few more times before he came. She swallowed all of him, reveling in the taste and the knowledge that she'd brought this large, hard, invulnerable man to his literal knees with her body and the pleasure she could give him.

It was an experience she would never pass up and never forget. That was a blessing and curse.

He continued to plunge inside, gentler now that he had come but riding out the aftershocks. She sucked on him, giving him as much of the last bit of pleasure his over-sensitized skin could handle. He pulled out on a low groan from them both as he slid down her body until they were face to face.

He traced his thumb along her bottom lip, his touch spreading the tingling warmth settling into her swollen flesh. His gaze studied her and she stared back, willing to let him look for whatever he needed and hoping he found it on some level.

Atticus closed the distance, his mouth taking hers in a deep, hot kiss that usually was reserved for the beginning of sex, but they were both still hungry. This had burned off a little of the edge but the combination of lust, danger, worry over Katrina, and adrenaline made it impossible to quench. At least for her—and the way he was possessing her mouth, it was the same for him.

"I can taste me and fuck that's hot," he murmured, breaking off the kiss.

"I love it," she answered honestly. There were few things she liked better. "I like you inside me, period."

This is what they did best. Sex had always been easy. Their compatible kinks, sex drive, desire to push boundaries, and trust had created a place where there was no shame and their needs would always be met.

For them, the physical had been easy to ask for and give. The emotional stuff outside of the bed had been their downfall.

"I like being inside you," he countered, giving her a flash of a grin before rolling off and flopping beside her on the mat. His long body was stretched out, long hair damp with sweat, his skin glistening and his shorts still pushed down. His cock lay on his thigh and she licked her lips at the sight. He caught her and let out a low, dark moan. "Don't even start with that shit. I can't fuck you again. We've got to get going."

"Carla arranged for Paulo to be at the club in…" She looked at the clock on the wall of the gym space. "…an hour and a half. Private room so that we can interrogate him."

"We? Have you been studying interrogation techniques while you've been gone?" he teased.

"I've got the most effective technique right here," she answered, gesturing with her hand down her entire body. "One look at me and he'll spill it all."

Atticus's expression darkened as he scowled at her. His voice was low and firm when he spoke. "He's not going to touch you. If he even looks at you sideways, I'll end him."

She stared at him, her entire being responding to his tone and her brain screaming, *If you feel that way then why can't we be together?* He was infuriating and confusing and she wasn't up to asking the questions she'd need to ask to get the answers she wanted from him. She didn't want to have to pull them out of him anyway. She'd spent her whole life virtually begging at the table of her parents and brothers for the words or the affection that should have been freely given.

She wasn't begging this man because the only way she'd know it was true was if he told her on his own.

Olivia stood and zipped up the front of her sports bra, turning to humor to end this situation without saying something stupid. "Well, let's get going then. If I get bored I might have to break into your wall safe to save my sanity."

The look of horror on his face was worth the price of admission.

Chapter Nine

"What exactly is this place?" Brant asked, his eyes roaming over the private room at Club D.

Rush scanned the faces all turned in his direction around the space: Brant, Jade, and Jake. They all stood around the space, firearms drawn and at the ready against the backdrop of the large four-poster bed and floor-to-ceiling mirrors on two walls. It was elegant and expensively decorated but simple. This was a room where people came to fuck, after all.

Carla spoke up from where she lounged on the sofa with Livvy. "Club D is a private club for couples and select singles who enjoy *the lifestyle*. We have extensive grounds complete with an indoor and outdoor pool and hot tub area, a restaurant, a private entertainment club, and numerous private playrooms for the guests to reserve and enjoy."

"What exactly is 'the lifestyle'?" Jade asked, only curiosity and no judgment in her question.

"We are more commonly, and incorrectly, called 'swingers,'" Livvy added. "But it involves more than wife-swapping and orgies in suburbia. The lifestyle is for people who want to be in committed relationships but also have the freedom to experiment with sex, but also just enjoy hanging out with like-minded people for social gatherings."

Brant turned to look at Rush and he knew what was coming next. "Were you a member of this club?"

"I still am, along with Livvy and Carla." He bit back a laugh at the surprise on his friend's face. "I met Livvy at a lifestyle resort in the DR. We joined this place together."

"And you didn't have any issues with your security clearance?"

He shrugged. "As I explained to them, my lifestyle is only a problem if someone can blackmail me with the knowledge. I don't publicize it but I don't give a fuck who knows what I like to do in bed." And he cut him off with the next question. "And before you ask, I like to fuck in public with my partner and in groups."

"So do I," said Livvy, her gaze moving to Carla. "She's a dedicated third."

"I join in when couples want a third to play with for a time." She stood, her curvy body rising up from the cushions and her long, dark hair swinging down her back. The very high heels she always wore gave her an illusion of height she didn't possess, but everything about Carla gave off a confident vibe. She was a respected psychiatrist in DC with a successful practice. "I'm also on the board of directors and if word gets out that I helped you guys with this little ambush, my ass would be out of here. So I'm going to go and leave you to your work. Paulo is on the property getting a massage. He should be done in about five minutes and I've left word for him to come here."

Livvy rose and gave her a hug. "Thank you so much. We'll make sure to take him out the private exit."

"I know you'll be discreet." Carla gave her a quick kiss on the cheek. "Call me before you leave for dinner or some play time."

Rush nodded as she moved to leave the room. "Thank you again, Carla."

"I'd say anytime but…let's not do *this* again. Okay?" She nodded her good-byes to the rest of the crowd and slipped out the door, leaving the room in silence. Whether or not it was awkward, he couldn't tell. Nothing about this place or what happened here embarrassed him but it did make some people uncomfortable. He figured that it was their shit to work out and he focused on what they were here to do tonight.

"Armed security is not allowed on the club side of the property, so Paulo should be alone, and while I hate to presume that he'll be unarmed, most people wear little to no clothing here so I'm not sure where he'd stash it if he had it."

"Are these rooms soundproof?" Brant asked.

"Yes, but for sex and not for gunshots, so let's try not to fire our weapons if we can help it," Rush said. "If he starts yelling before we can get the information out of him, we'll have to gag him or knock his ass out and do this elsewhere."

"You seem to think he'll cave fairly easily," Jade added, adding a silencer to her weapon with a wink and knowing grin.

Rush grinned back. He liked her and all the people Brant had assembled. They were trained and didn't balk at what needed to be done, even the shitty stuff.

"Paulo Guzzi is a pussy. He lives off his daddy's money and dabbles in being a criminal. It's one of the reasons that Figueroa uses him here in DC, easily manipulated and no real power base of his own. He's got paid security but no organization around him even though he thinks he's a big deal."

"He has extensive property in the area, in the Hamptons, and in Miami, as well as a yacht and a house on Lake Como. Lots of places for him to hide a young girl," Livvy added from her seat on the couch. She looked sexy in a slouchy, long T-shirt dress that slipped off one shoulder. He wanted to walk over and bite the exposed, tanned skin and then lick his way down her body. This afternoon had been fun, amazing, and now he wanted more. Needed more. He thought he saw *more* in her expression as they fucked, but then she'd walked away on a joke and since emerging from her shower had been the same easy-going Livvy he knew.

Warm and accessible but guarded as well. He knew he hadn't put the wariness in her eyes, that had been her life and childhood, but he'd only seen it fade when they were married, and then it had come back tenfold when things had all fallen apart.

He'd dreaded seeing her again, expecting fireworks and anger, but it had been okay, almost like the time in their early days when they'd enjoyed each other's company, fucked every chance they got, but were still strangers with no investment between them. And while he was glad she wasn't trying to kill him, it didn't feel like it was enough.

He shook all this shit with Livvy off, getting his head back in the fucking game. He'd fought against actually having her here. If Paulo got violent and things went downhill he didn't want her in the middle where she could get hurt. Fuck, if that wasn't his worst nightmare.

He also didn't want her to see him do his job. His real job. The one where he killed people without regret because he had to and he could. The one where he was anything but the hero they trotted out for photo ops when he'd worn the uniform. If most of the people knew what he'd been ready and willing and able to do when he'd gone into the zone, they'd take away his medals and ship him off to a secure facility.

But you sure as fuck couldn't complete the mission if you were dead and he always wanted to complete the mission. No exceptions.

He looked down at his watch. It was almost time.

"Jade you take point behind the door. Brant and I will be on the sides. We want him to see Livvy first and come all the way inside and get the door closed before we take him. Understood?"

They all signaled that they understood the plan and got into position just as a light knock sounded on the door and Paulo stepped inside. He wore a robe, was barefoot, and his grin at the view of Livvy was pervy enough to make Rush itch to shoot him on sight.

Jade pushed the door closed behind him and slid the lock just as Brant grabbed him and put him in an armlock. Rush moved into position and slid his gun into his mouth just as he was about to yell. The resulting sound was a muffled shout and a very distinctive whimper.

"Hey, Paulo, remember me? You can just nod since your mouth is full." He waited while Paulo nodded slowly, still struggling against Brant as he slid the plastic wrist restraints on him. "Good boy. Now, you're going to stop trying to get away and you're not going to yell for help. You got me? If you do, then I will put this gun back into your loud piehole and blow your tiny brain all over the wallpaper. Are we good? You can nod again."

Paulo paused for a moment, considering his options, but when Rush pushed the gun in a little deeper and his eyes welled up with tears when he gagged on it, the nod came quickly.

"Good boy. Now sit." Rush motioned toward the chair and Brant shoved him down in it. The man's robe flopped open, revealing his flaccid, uncut cock to everyone in the room. "Dude, fix your junk. Nobody wants to see that."

Paulo squirmed his lower body, moving his legs to force the fabric to cover himself. When he looked up at Rush, who'd sat down on the coffee table in front of him, he spat out a number of curses in Italian. Rush knew enough to catch every other word.

"Shut the fuck up, Paulo. I don't even know what you're saying and I don't care." He leaned in close, making sure his prisoner could see his gun at all times. "My friends and I are here to discuss where Figueroa has the girl stashed."

"I don't know what you're talking about," the man sputtered, trying his best to keep the tremor out of his voice. Rush gave him kudos for the effort. It wasn't easy to maintain your dignity when you were outnumbered. But he just couldn't deal with the lying. He stood, grabbed Paulo's face, and shoved his gun back inside his mouth. Rush ignored Livvy's gasp and plowed forward.

"I don't have time to go through this whole song and dance. You want to pretend you don't know and I'm going to have to spend hours getting you to tell me, and the only result will be that you will tell me and then spend days in the hospital while they repair the damage I will do to your face and your mouth and the internal organs you can spare. Believe me, I know how to do it all and I know how to keep a man alive and in as much pain as he can stand without passing out." He leaned in close and made sure Paulo saw only him in his line of sight. "So, why don't you keep your teeth and your spleen and tell me?"

He removed the gun and Paulo spat at him. Rush jumped back out of range but backhanded his prisoner at the same time. Blood poured from Paulo's nose and he groaned in pain.

Rush grabbed his face and forced him to look at him. "Listen, you slimy motherfucker. If you don't tell me where she is being held, I deposit you at Figueroa's doorstep and tell him that you offered the details on the Linchky deal to me for a price."

Rush really had no idea the full extent of the deal, but it had been one of the most recent dealings Elena had found on the hard drive between Hickman, Figueroa, and Guzzi. The widening of Paulo's eyes and his immediate sniveling and crying told him he'd hit pay dirt.

"He'll kill me if you do that," Paulo whined, his body shaking with his terror. Rush didn't blame him. Figueroa was not a nice guy to his friends, and his enemies were constantly disappearing. Rumors were that he had a guy on payroll who did nothing but make sure you begged for death at the end.

"Well, then tell me where the girl is and he'll never find out from me that you told. I'll get her back and make sure there's no connection between us."

Yeah, he was making a deal with a minion of the devil but his soul was already beyond saving, so what did it matter? Brant wasn't happy. He could tell by the shadow on his expression but that's why he'd brought him in. To do the dirtiest of the dirty work. At the end of all this, MacKenzie would have enough to send to whatever authority they wanted and make the world a better place.

Paulo stared at him and Rush could almost see the little hamsters in his head running at breakneck speed. He waited, knowing the silence would help raise Paulo's panic and bring him to the right decision faster. He knew the minute they'd won when Paulo's eyes cast downward, defeat weighing on his frame like lead.

"She's in a cabin I own in western Maryland," he said, his voice low and filled to the brim with fear.

"Good boy." Rush stood and patted him on the head, looking at Brant with a grim smile. "We found her, now let's go get her."

Chapter Ten

The dream was really good.

It was their honeymoon. Four days in the little casita in Mexico. Sand. Waves. Sun. Very little clothing in or out of the bedroom. His smile. Atticus wearing a full-on grin. As rare as pearls in an oyster.

Olivia stretched out on the couch, grabbing the throw as it slid off her body. The steady pump of the air conditioning had chilled the air and goose bumps rose on the skin exposed by her sundress. She rubbed lightly at her arms and blinked away the heavy cast of sleep on her eyelids.

The team had returned from Club D, armed with all the information they needed and formulated a plan into the wee hours. Using satellite technology and plats of the land and plans for the cabin hacked off various servers, they figured out how they would get in and get Katrina out. It had been exhausting to watch them argue every point, calculate distance and ammunition and plans B, C, and D just in case Plan A didn't work. They discussed the contingency for casualties and agreed that anyone injured would be left behind if it hindered getting the little girl out safely.

It had been a long, silent moment where her heart had stopped as everyone agreed, their mouths set in thin, grim lines. It had scared the living shit out of her.

Paulo was being held at his home by another member of the team and would be until the mission was done. And then they'd all settled in to catch a couple hours of sleep before they headed out before dawn, hoping to catch the kidnappers when they would least expect it.

A glance at the clock told her it was three in the morning and another look around displayed the various bodies crashed around the room. Jade Jax was draped across the other couch, an arm covering her eyes. Brant was lying on his back on the rug, arms crossed on his chest like Dracula. The other three men brought here as part of the rescue team were lying on the floor, soft snores rising up from their prone bodies. There was no sign of Elena but there was another couch in Atticus's office.

Atticus. Where was he?

She sat up, scanning the room. His all-too-familiar bulk was nowhere to be found. Olivia eased off the couch, shivering a little at the slight chill of air against the bare skin of her legs and shoulders in the sundress. Rubbing her hands over her arms, she moved around the side of the sofa and allowed her eyes to adjust to the dark as she scanned the room. Walking over to the stairs leading to the basement, she zeroed in her ears to pick up any sounds of him from below.

Nothing.

Turning, she peered out onto the deck and saw him. Or at least the top of his head over the back of a chair on the deck, the silhouette of his hand lowering a cigar from his mouth. The moon was high behind him, shining into the room and casting a silvery cast to his dark hair.

Olivia moved forward, her steps silent as she tiptoed across the hardwood floor. The door slid open on a soft hiss, the brush of her skirt mimicking the sound when she eased through and stepped out onto the deck. The door closed behind her as she saw his head cock to the right in silent inquiry.

"Are you okay?" she asked, scanning his features and trying to figure out his mood.

"Just trying to get shit straight..." He pointed at his temple. "...up here."

Oh. She was intruding on his time to prepare for what he had to do tonight. She moved to go back inside but his hand shot out and grabbed her wrist, holding her in place.

"You don't need to leave." A couple of long beats passed before he whispered, "Stay."

"Are you sure?"

All she got was a solid tug in his direction and she followed it, standing beside the lounger where he was stretched out. He looked up at her and the dark, silver-tinged depths of his eyes drew her in and spurned her to act on impulse. In a flash she'd swung a leg over and lowered herself over his legs, straddling his body. Her form blocked the moonlight from directly exposing his expression but she was close enough to see him clearly.

He looked tired already. The lines on the edges of his eyes and mouth were deeper than usual. She reached up and pushed his hair back from his face.

"You should be sleeping."

"I slept for about an hour. That's about all I get the night before a mission."

"Are you worried?" she asked, even though it was likely a stupid question.

"I'd be crazy if I wasn't." His eyes were glued onto her face, scanning her as if he was trying to memorize how she looked. "I sit and think about shit. Organize my gun safe. Recite the Greek alphabet."

"I always wondered…" Olivia thought back to the several times he'd gone out on deployment when they were together. She'd had to wait and wonder and fill in the blanks with her own imagination. "You never said anything."

He lifted the cigar to his mouth and drew on it. The silence wasn't uncomfortable but she sure as hell didn't know how to fill it. So she waited to see what he would do.

"You don't want to know what's in my head."

"I think…" She hesitated but decided to take the plunge anyway. If this was too much, she'd be gone tomorrow and wouldn't have to face down her embarrassment for long. "I think I do want to know. I always did."

He placed the cigar down on the table, balanced on the edge so that the ashes fell onto the deck. When he turned back to face her, his hands came up to cup her face.

"When are you going to stop slumming?" That took her back and she tried to flinch away, but he held her close. "What in the hell were you thinking getting involved with somebody like me?"

"As opposed to a man with a title? A castle? A trust fund?"

"Yeah. A guy like that."

She shrugged, debating on telling him the truth or just blowing it off with a joke or half-truth. But the fact that they'd never been honest with each other was what drove her batshit crazy about their past. Would they have had a chance if they hadn't kept all the secrets? If she'd told him from the beginning about her alter ego and if he'd told her…anything.

"You needed me. Not my money or my title or my connections…you just needed Livvy."

He stared at her for a few moments longer and then pulled her down, kissing her with soft brushes of his lips against her own. His stubble was rough against her flesh as his long hair tickled the bare skin of her arms. Her disappointment at his non-answer was fading with the increased pressure of the kiss, the sweep of his tongue inside.

And then he pulled back and pressed kisses along her jaw, ending with a gentle bite of her earlobe before he whispered, "The Navy gave me purpose but you gave me peace."

"I what? I did?"

"I've done so many horrible things. Awful things. Things I did for the right reasons but that doesn't mean they don't stay in my head." He pressed a kiss on her neck, nuzzling into her hair and then sighing on a deep exhale. His voice was roughened to gravel with his memories and the pain of all of them. She felt it like rough stones rubbed against her skin. She felt raw and could only imagine the damage they'd done to him after all these years. Inside him. "Just being around you made it stop. Turned off the constant replay."

"Are they in your head now?" she asked, her heart aching with the pain in his voice. Atticus never talked about this, never let her have any glimpse of what he carried with him. She'd known it was there, read the unknown stories in the lines on his face and the muttered anger of his nightmares. But he'd never really let her in. "Are they?"

"Turn them off, Livvy. I need to get my shit together to go save Katrina and I need some peace."

It wasn't "I love you"—he'd never said those words to her—

but it was close enough that her chest clenched in reaction.

She couldn't refuse. Would never refuse him. Olivia leaned forward and kissed his right cheek, then his left and finally pressed a sweet one against his mouth.

Her breath caught as he hooked a finger under the strap of her sundress and drew it down and over her shoulder, following its progress with the slide of his lips along her skin. He nipped and licked and sucked, leaving a wet trail that made her shiver in the slight chill of the early morning.

The shiver turned to fire racing along her veins when he drew a nipple into his mouth and pulled on it with a slow, sensual draw. She bowed back and offered her breast to him, silently begging him to take her deeper as she reached up to lower the other strap, exposing her entire torso to his touch.

Atticus took her invitation and roamed her body with his hands, the rough callouses on them dragging along some of her more sensitive spots and leaving behind sharp, tingling pleasure. He transferred his attention to her other breast, cupping it and scraping lightly against her nipple with his tongue.

"Are you getting wet for me, Livvy?" he asked, his words vibrating against her flesh. "I need to slide into your hot pussy and forget for a while. Only you…for a while."

Livvy could do this. She loved him, of course she could. Leaning in to kiss him, mimicking his earlier path as she trailed her own path of nips and licks along his jaw, burrowing under his hair to give his earlobe a bite and swirl of her tongue.

"I want you to fuck me out here. If the people inside your apartment wake up, they'll see us. Your neighbors could see us." She wove her fingers into his hair and pulled his head back, forcing him to look at her, the need building in her with each word. She'd missed this between them, missed being with a man who understood her deepest, darkest desires. To be seen as she was taken, to be touched by multiple partners and still want her for himself. She'd missed it, no other partner quite meeting her in the same place. They accommodated and dabbled a toe in the lifestyle but never embraced it like she had with this man. "I need it tonight, Atticus. Please."

In answer he stood, taking her with him, and she held on as her world tilted on its axis. He took several paces away from the lounger and placed her on her feet, keeping his large hands on her shoulders until she was steadied.

When he saw that she was okay, he stepped back and ordered, "Take off everything."

Chapter Eleven

He was so fucking lucky.

Rush licked his lips as Livvy did what he demanded, letting the dress slide to the floor at her feet and then easing her thong down her thighs and letting it fall to the ground as well. She stepped out of the pile and waited for him to give her the next direction.

He loved it when she was pliant, obedient. Rush wasn't a full-on dominant but when the mood struck them both, he loved to run the sexual show between them, and it made his cock hard as steel when she did as she was told.

Tonight he needed the edge of control. The past forty-eight hours had been one long test of his patience and ability to keep his shit together. To have the life of Katrina laid at his feet and to be forced to confront his never-ending obsession with his ex-wife had left him floundering and more edgy than usual.

And now with a mission just a couple of hours from happening, he craved an escape. And he couldn't think of a better way to escape than by burying himself inside Livvy.

Rush reached down and unfastened his belt, sliding the leather through the loops and dropping it to the ground with a soft thud and jangle of the buckle. Livvy's eyes tracked his movements as he unbuttoned the fly of his jeans and shoved them down just enough to allow his hard dick to spring free, sitting tight against his belly.

"Bend over the table," he said, jutting his chin toward the long dining table positioned in the middle of the deck. He watched as she did as she was told, bracing her body on her elbows and spreading her legs to give him a glimpse of the wet slick of her sex. "Don't move."

He glanced around the patio, the span of windows from the neighboring buildings. Some were lit in this early morning and her position would be in the perfect spot for them to be seen. His skin burned with the idea of it.

Rush reached into his back pocket and took out a condom, ripping the packet open and rolling it down his length. He took two steps forward and eased up behind her, running a hand lightly down her back and side, caressing the tight globe of her ass. Livvy shivered, a long slow one that undulated up and down her body, and he followed its path with his eyes, admiring the play of her sleek muscles under her skin.

"Keep your hands here," he directed as he ran his own down the length of her arms from her shoulder to her fingers. Grasping them, he eased them forward, bending her farther over at the waist, not flat against the tabletop, leaving space for him to feel the sway of her breasts as he fucked her. "Good girl."

Rush straightened, taking a deep breath as he shoved his jeans down a little farther, the chill of the night touching the exposed skin at the top of his ass. He moved between her legs and shoved them apart a little wider and then took himself in hand, easing his cock into her hot depths until he was fully seated.

"Oh my God, Atticus," Livvy gasped out, reaching behind her with her left hand to drag him even closer. Her nails dug into his thigh and he hissed with the sting he felt through the denim.

"I told you to keep them here." He grabbed her wrist and moved her hand back in place in front of her, pressing down lightly to make his point. "Hang onto the table while I fuck you, Livvy. I need you tonight."

She nodded, letting out a groan of frustration when he pulled almost all the way out. He looked down, gritting his teeth at the vision of him disappearing inside her once again, the sensation of her heat along his length. In and out, slowly and with control that caused sweat to run down his bare chest and his muscles to bunch with the effort, he maintained his pace until she panted under him.

"I'm going to...oh, fuck," Livvy said, her voice loud in the stillness of the early morning. "Oh, fuck...God save..."

She clenched around him with her orgasm and he picked up the rhythm, draping himself over her back as he pounded into her from behind. He braced himself with his left hand on the table, wrapping the other around her torso, cupping her breast in his palm. His thumb rubbed across the nipple, loving the press of the hard, pebbled flesh against his skin.

Rush leaned into her neck, nudging aside the damp fall of her hair to kiss her along her shoulder, punctuating harder thrusts with a bite that raised red marks on her pale skin. She pushed back into him, riding his cock now just as much as he was fucking into her. He wanted to wrap himself up in her, to crawl inside her and stay forever or as close to that time that people like him got.

He found himself talking, murmuring nonsense against her flesh. He knew he should shut the hell up but he couldn't have if his life depended on it. "It's never been like this with anyone else. I want everyone to wake up and see us, to know that you're fucking mine. *Mine*."

Livvy gasped at his words, her body jolting forward to lie flat against the table, pinned under his weight. She squirmed against his body, but her half-hearted attempts to shake him only made him hotter, harder. And it made his tongue looser, his need more primal.

"This pussy is mine. No matter who thinks they can take it, it's mine. Nobody makes you come like I do. Nobody gets you so wet it runs down your thighs. Nobody."

He looked down at her left hand clenched against the table and noticed that her finger was bare of his wedding band. The thought, only on his mind for the briefest second, hit him with such a force of anger and possession that he almost reeled back from it.

He lifted up and angled his hips in deeper, feeling the tingle of his orgasm in his balls, the small of his back. He was only going to get in a few more strokes before he blew and he wanted her to come again.

Lifting her up, he held her against his body, one hand supporting her as the other tangled in the wet curls covering her pussy. Fingering her clit, he stroked her, moving inside her at the same rhythm and never letting up until he felt her tighten around his cock, heard her loud groan as she came.

Rush shoved inside, his body taut with his own orgasm as he

emptied himself into the rubber. Thrusting in and out, he rode the wave until it was nothing more than a bolt of energy along his spine, adrenaline coursing through his system.

He pulled out and turned her around, stepping in between legs that she wrapped around his waist, keeping them as close as possible. The kiss was wet and hot, a clash of teeth and a parrying of tongues that echoed the current of just-shy-of-violent need zinging back and forth between them.

Livvy wove her fingers into his hair, pulling hard every time he tried to back out of the embrace, forcing him to stay when some part of him was screaming for him to run away, to keep some distance between them, and the other side was telling him to cut open his chest and let her see it all, to let her have it all.

What had started as a simple act of sex was becoming a storm he couldn't hope to escape. It was ripping every defense he had from his mind and his soul.

He couldn't be that raw going after Figueroa's men. Couldn't be that vulnerable. It would get him killed. It could get Katrina killed. Rush pulled away but Livvy wrapped her arms around his neck and held him close, her breath warm against his ear.

"I know you need to go but promise me one thing."

He nodded, unable to speak.

"Don't get shot tonight. Don't get hurt. It would kill me, Atticus. Just promise me that."

He nodded, swallowed hard and tried to clear the sawdust from his mouth. "I promise."

Livvy then released him and he stumbled back, pulling his pants up and heading to a shower and distance from her.

The Marines said that everyone had an Achilles' heel, the one thing that could get in your head and fuck with your game. Once you knew what it was, they said you could contain it, put it in a box when you needed to. They lied. Outright lied to his face because Livvy was his only weakness and nothing was more clear than the fact that he couldn't control it.

Chapter Twelve

"What the hell are you wearing?" Atticus said.

Olivia looked up as she entered the living area of the loft, scanning the room until she found him standing next to the long table, checking over his weapons. Several handguns, knives, and what looked like mini-grenades were laid out on the table, disappearing into the different slots all over his black tactical clothing.

She glanced down at her own outfit. All black, just like his, but in a body-hugging catsuit style. She wore it on some of her jobs and knew it was perfect for tonight.

"It's Dolce and Gabbana," she offered with a smile.

"You look like fucking Catwoman," he said, his face dark and unchanging when Brant snickered nearby. "Why the hell are you dressed like that?"

"For the rescue." She was confused. Wasn't it obvious?

"You're not going," Atticus said, dropping the magazine he was holding on the table and walking over toward her. He was pulled up to his full height of six feet five inches and looking down on her in an intimidating manner. She'd seen it before and it didn't scare her. "What could have possibly made you think you were going?"

Anger rose in her gut at his stupid question. "I've been a part of this from the beginning and I want to see it through with the team."

He was shaking his head before she even finished. "No. You

can see it through here. We'll let you know the minute we have her safe."

"I'm going," she said, stopping him with a hand to his chest when he meant to turn his back on her and go back to what he was doing. Atticus glanced down at her hand and then back up, his jaw tight with anger and frustration. He could join the club and get over it because she was feeling the same thing at his attitude.

"No. You're. Not."

She decided to change the direction. "Elena and Jade are going…"

He cut her off. "Elena will be in the communications truck, video monitoring the mission. Jade is a trained operative and has done this a million times before. You are very good at what you do but we don't need that skill set tonight. You need to be here."

"I can sit in the truck with Elena," she said, edging her voice in steel to make sure he knew she was serious about not being left behind. Not now. "I can know you're safe if I'm in the van."

His expression softened at her words and she tangled her fingers in the loops of his vest and dragged him closer. "I'm going with you tonight. You can't tell me no."

And like a flash of lightning across the sky, any tenderness was gone and it was replaced by resolute determination. It was like he slipped on a mask and obscured anything of the Atticus she knew and replaced him with a stranger.

"Livvy, I said no."

"I'm going."

"Don't tell me later that I didn't give you the option," he said, grabbing her around the waist and placing her in a fireman's carry before she could get out a protest. The world was topsy turvy and only ended with her deposited in the middle of his bed.

The bounce dislodged some of the hair from her ponytail. It flopped over her eye and obscured her vision. She flipped it back and attempted to scoot off the bed, but he grabbed her around the ankle and dragged her back to where he'd placed her.

"Atticus, let me go," she yelled, kicking out when he let go of her leg and reached for her hand. She nailed him in the gut and although he let out a grunt of surprise, it didn't slow him down.

A cool piece of plastic slipped over the hand he held tight in his grasp. She squirmed to look at it, recognizing the plastic wrist restraint too late to avoid him tightening it around her wrist.

"Atticus, you wanker. Don't you do this."

He stopped, holding her in place. His face was grim and determined. "Are you going to agree to stay here while we go to the cabin?"

She balked, hesitating a tad too long to be able to lie to him convincingly and he saw it. Olivia kicked out in frustration but it did no good. He was like a storm coming in from the ocean. All she could do was react to the inevitable.

He deftly grabbed her other wrist, looped the plastic restraint through the metal rungs on his headboard and slipped the open end over her hand. Three seconds of tightening and he was done and she was stuck.

"I can't believe you just tied me to your bed," she fumed.

"It's not the first time," he remarked, stepping back to stand by the bed. He was breathing hard, adjusting the gear she'd dislodged during her struggle. His expression was blank. He was already in the SUV and headed out to the kidnappers' location in his mind. He didn't care that she was furious. Not. One. Bit.

Cold-blooded bastard.

She was ass hurt because she had fooled herself into thinking this was different after the last few days. That maybe they were just different enough this time around to maybe get a second chance. Once again, she'd mistaken great sex and chemistry with this man as the foundation for a future. It hurt just as bad the second time around.

"I'll never forgive you for this," she growled out between clenched teeth, tugging uselessly against the restraints. She knew it wouldn't do any good but she did it anyway. Surrender was not an option she would take lightly.

"And I'd never forgive myself if you got hurt."

"You don't trust me." He didn't. Not like he trusted Jade or Elena.

"That's not important when it comes to your safety." He shrugged, reaching out to stroke her cheek, his face softer around the edges but she could almost see the rod of steel in his spine. She shook off his touch with a growl and a baring of her teeth, not wanting to get any kind of comfort from him.

Hurt crossed his face like a shadow as he straightened, backing toward the door. For a brief moment, she regretted her rebuff and almost called out an apology as the possibility that he might not come back. The fear was the only thing that cut through her anger for a moment.

"I'll have someone call Carla in an hour to come and cut you loose. I'll call you when Katrina is safe."

She watched him go, helpless to do anything but lay there and fume…and worry.

Chapter Thirteen

"I can't believe you tied her to your bed," Brant said, his glare as clear as day in the darkened SUV.

The rest of the team stilled and he could almost taste their desire to be anywhere but in the middle of this discussion. He didn't want to have it either.

Rush debated the merits of not answering him but he doubted that his friend would let it go. "She wouldn't agree to stay behind and I know just how stubborn she can be. She would've hired a cab to get her to the location. A decisive action had to be taken and I took it."

"Man, you're a cold son of a bitch sometimes."

He stiffened at the comment. It might be true enough in most instances but it was so far from the truth when it came to Livvy. She made him run too hot and wrecked his concentration. He answered the best way he could.

"These men are ruthless and they will not hesitate to kill Katrina if they get a chance…"

"I know that," Brant said, his irritation coating every word.

"I have to have my head clear, focused. I can't do that if I know that Livvy is within the range of danger. I need not to care about anything but making sure Katrina is safe and killing every dickhead that gets in my way." He took a deep breath and tried to rein in the desire to punch something or someone in the face. "I didn't have the time or the inclination to have a big fucking Oprah-talk with her about it. We were losing time and advantage and I did what I had to do. I'd do it again and if that makes me cold, then bundle up, motherfucker."

Silence filled the vehicle, the only sound their breathing and the clack of Elena's keys as she worked to hook up all the comm units and the satellite connection for global views of the site and infrared scans. She would be their eagle eyes when they were on the ground, giving him the information he needed in real time.

Rush bowed his head, getting his mind in the correct headspace. Running through the plan over and over, checking every detail against his training and his gut. The plan was solid and it should go off with only minor adjustments in the heat of battle.

They knew from early recon that there were three men on the grounds and three inside at all times. They had significant firepower and they carried themselves like professionals. This wouldn't be easy, but it was feasible with the team he had in place tonight.

They also knew Katrina was being held at this location. Paulo had been there the day she'd been taken, ensuring that Figueroa's men and the girl had adequate provisions for their stay. Everything for a successful rescue was in place and now they just had to execute.

His mind drifted back to Livvy and their time together in the early morning hours. Having her in his arms again had been the most tranquil moments he'd had in the three years since they split up. She was his center, his true north, and while he knew he'd crossed over a line tonight, he couldn't regret what he'd done. Knowing she was safe was the most important thing in his life.

He wasn't a praying man but he was superstitious when it came to going into battle. A prayer he'd learned in boot camp stuck with him and he recited it in a low voice:

"Lord, make me fast and accurate, Let my aim be true and my hand faster than those who seek to destroy me. Grant me victory over my foes and those that wish to do harm to me and mine. Let not my last thought be, if only I had my gun; and if today is truly the day you call me home, let me die in a pile of empty brass."

He thought he heard a quiet "amen" from the other side of the vehicle as it came to a stop a mile away from the location, parked in a dark copse of trees just off the road. They waited, scanning the area before filing out as quickly and quietly as possible. Once they were all in a circle, he went back over the high-level mission plans.

"The goal is to rescue Katrina and get her out unharmed. Eliminate anyone who would harm her or you. They won't hesitate to kill you."

They'd debated whether they would kill or just incapacitate the men they found here and Rush had insisted on elimination. He wasn't taking any chances. He'd seen Figueroa's men in action before and it was a good thing to take them out of the picture for good before they could do anything worse to anyone else.

He continued his instructions. "Brant and I are going in the front, Jade and Seth take the western side of the house, and Curt and Mike the east and go in the back door. Whoever gets to her first, remove her from the house and bring her here. We'll give you cover and secure the location. Understood?"

They all rogered agreement and headed out through the woods, leaving Elena to man the communications unit. They covered the mile quickly, seeing the cabin come into view just as the blush of sunrise was cresting on the horizon through the trees. It would have been a sight to stop and admire if they'd been here for pure enjoyment.

He held his fist up when they all reached the last bank of screen before the cleared driveway and yard of the cabin. Everyone stopped in perfect unison, their training evident. He motioned for the teams to split up and cover their areas. He hung back with Brant, giving the others time to get into position.

He looked at Brant, nodding toward the house. "You ready?"

"Hell, yeah."

"Let's go." Rush hunched down and moved silently and quickly across the field with Brant mirroring his movements. They'd worked together enough that hand signals sufficed when they needed to communicate and otherwise, they functioned as one.

He came across his man just as Brant grabbed his and Rush grasped the man on each side of his face and gave a twist, listening for the familiar sickening crunch of bone and spinal cord, dropping the guy to the ground. He patted down the body and took his weapons, stashing them on his person before looking over to find

Brant doing the same. They made eye contact and he motioned them forward.

There were two more on the porch of the house who gave more of a fight when they grabbed them. The scuffle of boots on the wood was loud enough to alert people inside and Rush cursed under his breath, pressing harder against the guy's pressure point until he slumped to the ground. He removed his Glock with the silencer on it and shot him once in the chest and once in the head. If they guy got up from a double-tap, he was fucking Dracula and Rush was no vampire slayer.

He slid over to the window and looked inside. Two men sat at a table in the kitchen playing cards while one stood in the doorway, keeping watch into the other room. They were all joking around, fucking off, but he wasn't fooled. They were professionals and could get their shit together pretty fast when they needed to.

He didn't see Katrina anywhere but Brant waved him over to a window on the opposite side of the door and he eased his way to him. Brant pointed and Rush looked inside, his breathing stuttering at the sight of Katrina lying on the couch in a ball, asleep.

Thank God. She looked unhurt.

Another man stood on the other side of the room, scanning the front and back areas, his weapons at the ready. He would be the one to take out first.

"We both go in. You take out the guy to the left and then the one on the right and I go for Katrina, yeah?" he asked Brant.

"Roger that." Brant tapped his earbud and spoke in a low voice, barely above a whisper. "We have visual on the girl. Four in the house that we can see. Are you in position?"

Affirmative responses were received from the two other teams. Rush moved into position at the door, ready to kick it in when Brant gave the signal.

"We're going in on the count of three. One. Two. Three."

Rush kicked at the door, the spot right above the keyhole, with the heel of his boot and the wood splintered, the door flying open. He moved forward, weapon aimed for the man standing to the right. He pulled the trigger and watched him flail and fall to the ground.

"Cover me," he yelled as he sprinted for the now-awake

Katrina, who was screaming and had fallen to the floor and skidded behind the couch and out of his sight. "Katrina, stay down!"

She stood anyway, fear igniting her "flight" urge, and he saw her emerge from behind the sofa just as a fifth man descended the stairs with his weapon drawn and aimed. Rush ran across the space, vaulting his body over the sofa as he watched the confused man focus on Katrina and then himself and then back at Katrina as he lifted his weapon to shoot. He probably had orders not to hurt her but he was reacting to the situation and she was in his sights.

Rush got to her, shoving her down to the floor under his body just as the first shot ripped through his shoulder, followed by another a little lower. The pain sliced through him but he took his aim with his gun. Before he could get off a shot, Brant took the man down in a hail of bullets.

He huddled over Katrina's shaking body and scanned the area, looking for additional men to come out of the woodwork. In the back of the house he could hear shouts as the rest of the team secured the building. Brant came into view, concern written all over his face as he dropped down beside him.

"Christ, Rush, you've been shot," he said as he pulled back Rush's shirt and gear to see the wounds. "Fuck, twice."

"It always hurts like a motherfucker."

"Rush?" Katrina's small, scared voice ripped him out of his haze of pain as she squirmed out from under his weight to wrap her arms around him and bury her face against his neck. "Rush, you came to get me."

"Fuck, Kit-Kat, you knew I would," he ground out between his clenched teeth, wholly unconcerned that he was cussing in front of her. "Did they hurt you?"

"No," she said, the tears starting in earnest now and soaking his skin and mingling with his own sweat. She hugged him harder and he saw stars as she pressed against the wound that Brant was trying to compress as he called Elena for the SUV. "They kept saying that somebody would be mad if I was damaged. They weren't supposed to hurt me."

He closed his eyes in relief as he muttered a "thank God" under his breath. The room swam around him and he realized that his entire front was soaked in blood, his blood. It was coming out pretty fast and he could already feel the effects. Rush forced his eyes open and locked gazes with Brant.

"Katrina, you're going to need to go with Mr. Scott, okay?"

She shook her head and latched on tighter, refusing to look at him or anyone.

"Yeah, you need to go with him because I'm going to pass out and squish you in about five seconds."

He had less than that as he felt the world fall away from beneath him, his last thought that he'd broken his promise to Livvy.

Chapter Fourteen

Even wearing one of the ridiculous hospital gowns, Atticus still looked invincible.

And sexy.

In fact, he was the best thing she'd seen in a very long time.

The IV hooked to his arm and the beeping machines assured them all that he was breathing and all his organs were working like they should. The staff had attempted to clean him up as best they could but he still had streaks of dark red across his collarbone and right cheek. He was a little pale under the dark tone of his skin but he looked better than he had a couple of hours earlier. A couple bags of blood made a huge difference and she was finally able to breathe deeply.

The time between the phone call telling her he'd been shot and when the doctor gave him the "all clear" had taken years off her life. At least a full decade. For the time it had taken Carla to drive her to the hospital, her heart had stopped beating at least a dozen times and she'd worried that he was also gone and her body somehow knew. She *never* wanted to feel that way again.

Her anger at being restrained and left behind was still there but the fear of losing him and subsequent exhilaration of knowing he would be okay had watered down the fury to a dull, resigned thud. He was Atticus and he would never change. He wouldn't explain and he wouldn't talk to her. Trying to get him to change was as futile as a caged bird beating its wings and thinking it could fly.

Olivia shifted in the moderately comfortable chair, stretching her neck and back. She picked up the cup of coffee, took a sip and grimaced at the cold beverage before leaning over to toss it into the trash. Glancing at the clock on the wall, she eased out of the chair and walked to the window, gently pushing aside the blinds to look at the DC skyline shining white and gleaming against the dark backdrop of the night sky.

"You had a chance to zip-tie me to the bed and you missed it."

Olivia's heart stuttered and then thudded against her chest. She reached out and steadied herself against the shallow window ledge, a brief press of her suddenly heat-flushed flesh against the cool of the window glass.

"A lady never kicks a man when he's down."

"The Queen would be proud." The sharp inhale of breath from Atticus as he shifted behind her prompted her to move to his side. Olivia reached out, hands hovering over him since she was unsure about the help he needed from her. Knowing Atticus, he didn't need, or want, anything from her.

"What can I do?"

"I'm good. I'm good," he insisted as he moved slowly, inching into a sitting position. She motioned toward the controller, which would elevate the head of his bed, and he gave a quick nod. She pulsed the button and the mattress shifted upward.

"Thank you." He looked down and picked at the IV tubing and growled. "This is ridiculous. It was just a flesh wound. I've had worse."

"It was more than a flesh wound and the nurse said you lost a lot of blood and they were worried about your vitals." Olivia reached out and lightly brushed a finger over the white bandage spanning the area between his collarbone, shoulder, and upper chest area and then lifted it to the one covering the side of his head, dangerously close to his temple. "We were *all* worried when you wouldn't wake up."

She tried to head off the catch in her throat, to blink back the tears testing her waterproof mascara. But hell, he'd scared her. The thought of losing him… Atticus wasn't part of her life, but the thought of a world without him in it made her blood run cold and her heart calcify.

"It will take more than some Colombian assholes to end me,"

he murmured, his own hand reaching up to capture hers as she lowered it. The unspoken words—*please don't cry on me*—hovered in the air between them. They stared at each other for a few moments and she found it impossible to read whatever was going on in his mind. As always. But she wanted to know, wanted to be the one he told things so that she didn't have to guess. She wanted to be the one he *wanted* to tell.

He opened his mouth to say something and Olivia withdrew her hand, breaking their connection. Turning toward the attached bathroom, she grabbed a clean washcloth and filled a basin with warm water. When she came back into the room he was watching the door, his expression equal parts suspicious and curious.

"What are you doing?"

"Relax, I'm going to clean off some of the blood. You look like a train wreck." She placed the basin on the tray next to his bed, dampened the cloth and began to dab at the smears on his cheek. He watched her, his gaze intense and when he spoke, his voice was rough with the gravel of battle and fatigue.

"How is Katrina? The team? Are they okay?"

"They only had very minor cuts and scrapes. Katrina is at home already. She was unharmed except for being scared half to death and a little dehydrated." Olivia met his gaze. "Brant and the others had to leave when visiting hours were over but I lied and told them that we were still married so they would let me stay."

He looked confused. "Aren't you pissed at me?"

She scoffed. "Furious, actually. I want to shove your face down into the water and drown you."

"So…you *are* mad."

She gave him a sharp look as she rinsed and wrung out the cloth. "Don't make fun of me, Atticus." She felt the break in her voice before it happened and no matter what she did, she couldn't hold it back. "Just. Don't."

"Livvy." His tone dipped deeper into the pit of gravel and her eyes prickled with tears caused by the last few hours, few days. The heavy weight of new and old emotions from the past threatened to bring her down, and for once she was glad she'd taken off her heels before curling up in the chair because she wasn't entirely sure she could stay on her feet otherwise.

"It doesn't matter. I can be as mad as I want but it won't change who you are and that you think you did the right thing. You're not sorry you tied me up." He paused and she eyeballed him. "Are you?"

He shook his head, his expression somber but not contrite. "No. I'd do it again."

"Because you don't trust me."

"Because it was a dangerous situation and two nights ago I told you to get out of the house and you took out your earbud, ignored me, and almost got caught. I couldn't take that risk with a bunch of kidnappers with guns."

"I didn't follow your orders at the senator's house because I had it all under control." She tossed the cloth onto the side table and pointed at him. "Do you know how many times I've been in that same exact situation? I wouldn't tell you how to do your SEAL stuff because I trust you to know how to do *your* job. B&E is my job."

But this issue keeping the gulf between them was more than a simple theft job. He didn't trust her. Not really. She'd lied to him and he'd put up walls and that was the beginning, middle, and end of that story. There was nothing she could do and nothing she could think to say that would change it.

"Livvy."

He reached out to touch her but she dodged him, moving to the end of the bed. Letting him touch her was a very bad idea. Being within arm's reach of him for the last few days had been the worst idea she'd ever had. Having sex with him again? Epically stupid.

"I'm going home, Atticus. Tonight. I was just waiting for you to wake up to say good-bye."

He stared at her and she waited for him to tell her to stay. To say he didn't want her to go. To say he would miss her and maybe they could talk soon? That they could start over and...

But that was a joke. This was the guy who'd never given her the chance to explain about her past, about the stealing, to do anything to make it up to him. He'd written her off and they were done.

He'd been done.

She'd never be done. That much she knew.

"Katrina is back at home. You've got to get back to your mountain. I have things to do."

It was pathetic but she waited, watching him closely to see if she saw anything in his expression that would tell her to stay. He stared back at her. Silent and stoic as always. Giving nothing away and she had nothing more to give. He had it all.

He just didn't want it.

She rubbed her hands on her pants, looking around to locate her purse. She spied it on the floor and reached down to scoop it up, placing it over her shoulder. Olivia slid her feet into her heels, the boost making her stand up taller and uncover the strength to give him a smile.

She walked over to the side of his bed again, reaching for the damp cloth, surprised when he let her wipe gently along his collarbone. The blood came off easily but she got his hair wet in the process, so she pushed it back and finished the job. Her fingers got tangled in the strands of his hair and she enjoyed the slight wave of silk in her hands.

"For the record, I like the hair. The marauding dark Viking is a look you can pull off. Brant is just jealous." The joke fell flat even to her own ears and she pressed her lips together to keep from saying something worse.

He reached up as she pulled away, his fingers wrapped around her wrist. "I feel like there's something I should be saying. I just don't know what it is."

She pondered that for a moment, wondering if this was the opening she needed. But she couldn't feed him the words she wanted to hear. He'd never told her he loved her and that was a hard limit for her. The bottom line was that she needed him to say them because he couldn't go another minute without saying them, not because she gave him verbal prompts. They couldn't build anything on the real-life equivalent of mad libs.

But she knew what *she* wanted to say.

"We were never easy, Atticus. Not really. Sex was the only time we made sense and no matter how hard we like to pretend, that's not enough. I'm still me and you're still you and there is no natural place where we are going to meet in the middle." She took a steadying breath and continued, knowing that this would be her only chance to vent. "I think we had our moment to try and find a place to build a bridge and it passed many years ago. But I'm glad we got this time. I'm glad the way we ended before isn't our last memory of each other."

Three little words were poised on the edge of her tongue but she would not let them fall into the space between them. Olivia had said them before for nothing. Her utter humiliation at begging for him to take her back was burnt on her heart, and she wouldn't do it again. They were not the magic talisman as portrayed in books or movies, not the key to unlock the secret to happiness.

So she leaned forward and kissed his mouth. It was brief, light but also heavy with its finality. It was a good-bye kiss, after all. It should have some weight.

"Livvy, I…" Atticus rasped out the whispered words, his voice faltering with the words he couldn't, wouldn't, or didn't want to say. The regret was hard to miss but it wasn't what she needed to hear. She didn't want him to miss her; she wanted him to need her.

"Me too," she answered, leaving the rest unsaid as she turned to walk out of his room without a backward glance and shut the door.

The hospital corridor was as empty as she would expect at almost midnight. She nodded at the nurses behind the desk and tried to keep down the noise created by the tap of her high heels on the hard tile.

Olivia stopped at the elevator and pushed the down button for the main lobby. She'd grab a cab back to the Batcave, gather her bags and head straight to the airport. The sooner she got back to her regularly scheduled life, the sooner she'd tie up and shut down the feelings that had escaped their cell in the basement of her heart the last couple of days.

Chapter Fifteen

He did a double take when he saw who was standing on his front stoop.

The video monitor was filled with the face of Katrina Hickman, her huge eyes blinking in the bright sunlight, a bandage on her right temple. A big dude in a black suit and the stereotypical dark aviator sunglasses stood just behind her. He pressed the intercom.

"Yeah?"

"Let me up, Rush." She held up two wrapped gifts. "I have something for you."

Oh hell. She got him a gift? She looked up at the monitor, the smile on her face widening as she waved the boxes wildly back and forth.

Oh hell.

"Come on up."

He could hear the pounding of her feet on the stairs and opened the door just as she hit the landing. She stopped when she saw him, her eyes widening when she saw the bulky bandages under his T-shirt and the dark bruises on his face.

"Oh, Rush," she said and then flung herself at him, catching him around the waist with her thin arms.

He could hear her sniffling, imagine the tears running down her cheeks, and it took everything in him not to ditch her and run. But what he did surprised him. Reaching down, he grasped her around the waist and pulled her up until her arms could wrap around his neck and he squeezed her tight, letting her know that he was here until she worked this shit out.

Eventually her sobs died down and he braved a peek at her. Cheeks red and eyes slightly puffy, she looked done. Thank God.

"Oh, Rush." Her lower lip wobbled again and he unlatched her from his neck and slowly lowered her to the ground.

"Nope. No more of that. I'm fine," he said, nodding toward her bodyguard as he closed the door behind them. "Do your parents know you're here?"

"Yes." She rolled her eyes in tandem with the sarcastic answer and he looked at the bodyguard for the confirmation nod. When he got it, he motioned for her to continue inside. She wiped her cheeks and looked around the space, nodding in approval. "This is cool."

"Thanks." Rush almost mentioned that Livvy had helped him choose and decorate it but he bit it back. Just because his mind always strayed to her didn't mean his mouth had to follow.

It had been a long week since she'd left him in the hospital, and once the debriefs and post-mission crap were wrapped up with Brent, he'd had a lot of time to dwell on what would never happen. Too much time. So much that he'd sent out feelers on the network that he was available for jobs.

He returned his focus to Katrina. "How are you doing?"

"I'm good. Seeing a shrink and I have nightmares." Her honesty shocked him but she didn't notice and kept talking. "They say they'll get better."

"They do," he said, debating how honest to be with a young girl. After what she'd been through it would help for her to know what the deal really was. "They don't go away but they do get better, less frequent. You learn to deal with them."

Katrina nodded. "Thanks for being honest with me. All of the adults are telling me that I just need to sleep it off and then whispering behind my back. It helps not to hear the same old bullshit."

He considered correcting her cursing but he wasn't her dad. Instead he went with what he could do, but it shocked him to hear the words that came out of his mouth. "You've got my number. Call me if you need to talk."

"Anytime?" She waggled her eyebrows and he had to laugh.

"Stalker." She smiled and he let out a breath that he hadn't freaked her out. He didn't know shit about dealing with kids. "Do you want something to drink?"

"Can I have a soda?"

"Are you allowed to drink soda?"

"No."

He knew her mother was a health nut. Fuck it. This was his house. "Grape or orange?"

"Orange," she said, her smile wide and bright. He hid his own grin behind the open door of the fridge when he leaned in and grabbed a soda for her and a beer for himself. Handing them off, he motioned for them to head out onto the deck.

Katrina popped the top and slurped at the soda, skipping across the patio to look over the edge and across the view. He lowered himself into one of the lounge chairs and watched her. She was a good kid and he was glad to see her okay.

"Do you want your present?" she asked, turning to face him. In the bright light he could see bruises on her neck and wrists and he tamped down the rage at her markings. She was fine now.

This wasn't about him being pissed or the likelihood that her dad might be going down for corruption if Paulo tattled like the little bitch he was. Brant had made sure that the right people got the info on the stolen hard drive. Rush hoped she didn't hate him when it all went down.

Katrina sat down on the lounge next to him and held out the box. "I hope you like it."

"Do I lie if I hate it?"

"Of course," she said, nudging the box even closer. He took it, turning it over and over in his hands. She sighed and rolled her eyes. "It's not a bomb. Open it."

"Brat," he grumbled, ripping back the paper and exposing the gift. It was a frame and when he turned it over his breath caught in his throat. A drawing, a really great one. It was her. Smiling. Holding a dog. A yellow lab. That's what all the happy suburban families had these days. They fit in the back of their environmentally friendly SUVs. A big "thank you" was scrawled across the bottom. "You're a great artist, Kat. I'll hang it on my wall. Thank you."

It wasn't a lie. He could tell how much she'd improved over the last few years. He had no idea what all the lines and shading things were called but she had a talent. It was good. He nudged her with his elbow, biting back the wince when he strained the stitches in his shoulder.

"Is that mine too?" He nodded toward the other gift.

She shook her head. "It's for Olivia. I heard you would have never found me without her."

Okay, that surprised him. He schooled his expression to not show how much he hated that Livvy was gone. "Really? I thought she was your nemesis."

Katrina rolled her eyes. "I hate to tell you this but I've moved on. I have a boyfriend."

He forced himself not to laugh. You didn't laugh at girls when they were putting you in your place. He knew that much. He'd rarely gotten it right with Livvy but apparently this old dog could learn a new trick.

"Good to know." He placed the unopened present on the side table and picked up the beer. "I'll make sure she gets it."

Katrina turned on her chair and looked around the deck as if she expected Livvy to materialize in front of them like magic. If she could then he would have conjured her a million times already. But if wishes were horses…beggers would ride.

"She isn't here?"

"Nope," he lifted the bottle to his mouth and took a healthy swallow. "She left a week ago. I don't know where she went."

"Why isn't she here? You two were working together to save me. I thought…"

Apparently everyone had thought the same thing. Brant had chewed him a new asshole when he found out that he'd let Livvy leave. It didn't matter that Rush had had no way to make her stay.

"No, Kat. That's not how it works."

"Then explain it to me. I'm a kid."

A kid, my ass. He gave her the hairy eyeball. "If I was any good at it, I'd explain. But I'm not…good at this. I suck at it actually."

"You don't love her?" He took another sip from the bottle to avoid answering the question. Katrina was persistent. "I thought you *loved* her."

"We're divorced, Kat. That ends all that…love stuff." He'd never even told her how he felt. Words were not his thing. He'd done his best to show her but when it had mattered, he'd been an ass.

And then too chicken-shit to follow her and make it right.

It was like Katrina could read his mind. She whispered, her eyes locked on his own, "I didn't think you were afraid of anything."

He went completely still, staring at her. A little girl on the edge of growing up with a big-ass bandage on her face and bruises from being kidnapped by a psycho bunch of killers and she was looking at him with such overwhelming…disappointment.

Fuck. That stung.

"She's better off without me. We just make each other crazy."

"Then you figure out how to get along anyway. Crazy has to be better than the grumpy and miserable thing you are right now."

"I'm not…" He shut his mouth, the lies dying on his tongue. He was too tired to lie to anyone, including himself.

"You need to go get her back. She's your forever person and you need to make it right."

"My what?" Rush squirmed in his seat as her words hit a little too close to the truth.

"I see it on your face. You're not that good at hiding anything when it comes to Olivia. I knew that she was special the first time you mentioned her in a letter. All it said was, 'I went to a baseball game with Olivia' and I knew I was out of the picture."

He couldn't stop the snort at that one. Figures a twelve-year-old would be the one to hand him his ass. "You knew, huh?"

"Yeah and when I saw you two together that time? When you came back from Iraq?"

"When you froze us both out and acted like a brat?"

She nodded. "It was because you two looked like a couple. A real, in-love couple, and I was jealous." She poked him in the side and then grabbed a handful of his T-shirt, making sure he looked her in the eye. "You were happy. You didn't walk around with a big, stupid smile on your face but you were happy. The deep down kind that just makes your whole face look different. I've only ever seen that when you were with her. Don't you want that back? *Everybody* wants that. Don't you?"

Did he? Yes. Right down to his marrow.

He thought about what she said and he knew she was right. He'd been happy with Livvy and that had terrified him because it meant she had the power to hurt him. Life had convinced him that it was foolish to try and keep people in your life but had left him unprepared for the moment when someone wanted to keep *him*. That had been...everything and he'd fallen in love with her because of it. He still loved her for seeing something in him worth keeping.

Rush took another drink from his beer, hoping Katrina didn't see his hands shaking. "It's over now."

It was lame but it was all he could think of to say at this moment. He wasn't going to spill his guts to a twelve-year-old girl. Even one as smart as the one glaring at him with preteen indignation.

"That's not the same as saying you don't love her. I'm a kid and even I know the difference."

He wasn't a kid and he knew the difference too.

But did he have the guts to do anything about it?

Chapter Sixteen

When he'd really thought about it, it wasn't hard to figure out where Olivia had gone.

The cottage, surrounded by a walled garden, faced the small village green in Oxfordshire. The little place sat in the shadow of her family's estate just a few miles down the road. Close enough but not too close. Just the way Olivia would want it. She loved her family but she'd need a place of her own. A place where she could be herself—as fucked-up as that might be. One of the many things they had in common.

Rush parked the car and exited, nodding to the two older women walking their dogs. Their eyes bugged out, taking in his long hair, tattoos, black T-shirt, and jeans before scurrying off to the main part of the village, likely intending to call the cops and report the dark Viking who'd landed on the shores of Her Majesty's kingdom. He'd better grovel quick or Olivia might just let them cart him off to jail for the night.

He headed toward the door, his eyes scanning the brick façade and the wood-shingled roof, the windows open to accept the breeze cutting the heat of the day. A noise just over the wall caught his attention and he paused. Music. Singing.

Olivia was singing. Badly, as always.

It was one he recognized. The lyrics all about how the girl was kicking the shitty lover to the curb and they were never getting back together. He groaned, hands clenched in fists in painful reaction to the awful song and also the words. Olivia was going to bust his balls. Yeah, he deserved it but knowing the pain was coming didn't make it any easier to take.

Rush considered for a long moment walking up the path and ringing the bell. It would be the polite thing to do. The non-confrontational way to go. But he guessed that he'd never get past the front door if he asked the nice "pretty please" kind of way.

And that shit just wasn't his style.

Rush examined the wall, eyeballing the trailing vines, flowers, and foliage. He didn't want to squash her garden, but his best option was up and over. If this went the way he hoped, he could replant the stuff he ruined.

With some care, he found a spot of almost-bare brick along the wall, grabbed a hand and foothold on it, and hoisted himself up. Ignoring the twinge of pain in his other shoulder, he caught a glimpse of the surprise on Livvy's face when he hit the top but lost it in the blur of motion as he launched himself off the ridge and executed a perfect roll on the green lawn. He came up in a crouch and froze when she stood just outside of arm's length, her garden spade aimed at him with deadly intent.

The anger and surprise in her eyes matched the glint of the metal of the spade where the bright sunshine caught it. Her hair was snarled around her face in bright gold curls. She wore no makeup but her cheeks were pink with her effort and matched the soft fabric of her sundress. She was barefoot, her long legs, arms, and shoulders exposed and begging for him to take a taste. Or several. He swallowed hard and rose slowly, raising his hands defensively when she advanced on him.

Rush wanted to grab her, pull her down to the grass, and fuck her until she was limp beneath him and remind her how good they were together. But if he'd learned anything, it was that their issues weren't about sex. It was about more. The "more" that kept people together for fifty to sixty years. The kind of "more" he'd only seen at a distance in movies or with the MacKenzie clan. Rush had never had anything close to "more" but he wanted it.

With Livvy.

He dropped his hands and stood still in front of her. He spoke softly. "If you need to stab me with that thing in order to get to a place where you can hear me, go ahead."

She cocked her head at him as if he was an alien and she couldn't believe he spoke English. He waited. It killed him to do it but he waited. She needed to know that whatever happened next was up to her.

"What is this? It's been two weeks with no contact and you launch yourself over my wall and expect what? You must think I'm mad to think I'd buy anything you're selling." She stepped closer, keeping the spade in front of her. Her eyes scanned his body before returning to look at him straight on. "If you forgot the zip ties, I'm sure I've got some in the garden shed."

"No." He shook his head. "No. I came to say I'm sorry."

"What?" The hand holding the spade dropped a little with her shock but she corrected quickly. Always on guard. Always wary. The fact that she'd let her defenses down with him for a second time and he'd thrown it away cut into his gut as if she'd thrust her weapon in deep. The pain was real and he'd barely survived last time.

He hit the ground on his knees, hand splayed out before him in a gesture of surrender. He'd never bowed before anyone. Never acknowledged the power that one person could have over him. Yes, he'd pledged his allegiance to a country he loved and served. He'd stood with his brothers-in-arms and fought alongside them or in their memory. He was a fighter, a man honed from hard beginnings as a throwaway kid and sheer will and determination. He'd never needed anyone. He'd built a life that ensured he'd never need anyone.

But he needed her and life had taught him that some rare things were worth giving up the one thing you coveted most. His pride was nothing if it kept them apart for another moment.

The spade in her hand fell to the lawn with a dull thud. Her hands flew to her mouth but they couldn't prevent him from hearing her gasp of surprise.

"Atticus, what are you doing?"

"I'm begging."

"It's too…" she stammered, starting to lean forward to make him stand up, but he shook his head and she backed off. Her expression was equal parts pain and confusion. "This is too much."

"No. If this is what I need to do to get you to come back to me, then it's just enough."

"Come back to you?" That spooked her and she started shaking her head, her body now poised for flight. He could tell by the subtle change in the shift of her body toward the open space to his right and the door beyond. The way she stood on the balls of her feet, ready to run at the slightest provocation. He started talking, hoping it would keep her here long enough to change her mind. Or to make his escape if she went for the spade again.

He took a deep breath. "I love you, Livvy. I never stopped. I'm never going to stop. I know jackshit about love and marriage or anything normal but I won't fuck it up again if you give me another chance." Here was the hard part. Livvy would either believe him or not. "I left you behind not because I didn't trust you but because I didn't trust myself to keep my head in the game if you were there. I'm a soldier. A hired gun. People put me on the scent of a target and I go after it with deadly tunnel vision. I needed to keep that edge to survive, to make sure that my fellow soldiers and the girl we were trying to save stayed safe. But one thing the Marines taught us is that everyone has an Achilles' heel and you're mine. Because if I lost you…*really lost you*…I'd lose the only home I've ever known." He paused, reaching out to snag her fingers with his own, letting out a little bit of the pent-up energy in his gut when she allowed him to tangle them together. "For a kid who wasn't wanted from the moment he was born, I didn't think anyone would ever look at me and say 'mine.' I never allowed myself to want that, to need that, because it wasn't meant for me. But when I fell for you and you loved me back? That was a miracle moment. It was all my secret desires right there in front of me for the taking and even as I accepted it, I kept waiting for the other shoe to drop."

"So why did you throw it away? Why didn't you come after me?" Her voice was barely above a whisper but every syllable was as loud as a shout and as painful as a slap.

"Because I was arrogant and stupid. I was mad and then I was too fucked up to apologize, to try and work it out. I thought I could just move on and not deal with you and your personal brand of crazy." She opened her mouth to argue, her eyes narrowed with a flash of anger. "I forgot about the truckload of crazy I brought to the table. I let it matter when it should have been nothing. I knew it the minute you left. I knew it every time I checked on you to make sure you were safe. I was just too full of pride to go after you and tell you that I was wrong. To tell you that I wanted nothing more than to be yours again. That you were my home and that I need you."

Livvy stood, staring down at him with an expression he couldn't read. He waited, sending up a prayer to the patron saint of fuck-ups to make this right. Rush wanted to pull her close but he waited, hating every moment of helplessness.

"I think that's the most you've ever said to me at one time," she said, her voice so low that it almost disappeared on the breeze coasting through her garden.

"Jesus, Livvy, don't bust my balls over this. I'm not sure I can take it."

She paused the briefest of seconds before asking, "I'm your home?"

"You're the only home I've ever had." He swallowed hard, clenching his hands in an effort to stop the shaking. "I love you."

She dropped to her knees in front of him, tears running down her cheeks, smearing the smudges of dirt she had on them from working in the garden.

"You never said it before."

"If you give me a chance, I'll never stop saying it."

Livvy nodded, her breaths mingling with her sobs and laughter as he reached up and cupped her face and pulled her in close.

At the last minute she whispered, "I love you."

This kiss wasn't like any other they'd ever had. It tasted like a future, belonging, and love. And a whole lot of wicked desire. The best combination, in his opinion.

She broke it off first, her eyes scanning his face, the area between her eyebrows scrunched with concern. "About my extracurricular activities…"

"I'm not crazy about you being in danger and risking your neck with this stealing gig but we'll work something out." He nipped her bottom lip, his fingers busy untying the thin little straps of her sundress. He needed her. Desperately. "There's got be a way for you to not risk a felony conviction and still let you steal things."

She laughed, her hand flying up to cover her mouth. He stopped what he was doing to ask, "What?"

"Remind me to tell you about my job offer." She leaned in for his kiss, her smile sexy and enough wicked to make his breath catch in his chest. "Later."

Epilogue

One year later. Paris.

You could see the glow of the glass pyramid from where he parked the car.

The streets were dark with only the streetlamps casting pools of yellow light on the ground. Some people still walked around, the usual crowds reduced to couples walking hand-in-hand as the evening slid into the darkest part of the night. He cut the engine and turned to Livvy, biting back his laugh at her confused expression.

"What are we doing here?"

"I'm going back to our hotel and you're going to break into that building and see if you can steal a painting and ask her first hand why she's smiling."

Livvy hadn't been speechless often in the last year, never afraid to tell him what she wanted and what she didn't. If the first time they'd been together had been largely silent, this time around was the complete opposite. There was nothing off the table, nothing that couldn't be discussed or shared. He still wasn't chatty but he made sure she knew what was important. Like the fact that he loved her. Worshipped her. Always wanted her.

He told her all the time. And she told him the same and he never got tired of hearing it.

And now he got to hear it for the rest of his life. Married for the second time just two short days ago, he was just now delivering her wedding present. One he'd cooked up with a lot of help from Brant.

"I get to break into the Louvre? Are you kidding me?" She unfastened her seatbelt and was bouncing in the leather seat, her eyes bright with excitement. "Are. You. Kidding. Me?"

"Nope." He grunted out a laugh as she crawled over the center console and straddled his lap. She laced her arms around his neck and he lifted his hands to run along the bare skin exposed by the back of her dress. Soft and silky and warm to the touch, his fingers itched to undo the few buttons that secured the dress and bury himself in her body again. "Brant is helping them with the new laser security system you assisted him with and he made sure you got to test it first. Why do you think I insisted we come to Paris for our honeymoon?"

She'd wanted to hide out at the Montana cabin, a place she'd fallen in love with over the past twelve months. They divided their time between it and her homes in England and Mexico, but she'd fallen in love with the mountains and preferred to be there more often than not. Rush was fine with it. He got to have her all to himself when they were there. It was a perfect.

"And I can steal her? Really?" Livvy licked her lips, her breasts against his chest and rising and falling with her excitement. Rush caressed the side of her body, his thumb flicking over the tight nipple under the silk of her dress just to hear the little catch she always made in the back of her throat.

"Yeah, baby. You can steal her," he growled, leaning in to take her mouth in a deep, thorough kiss that was over way too soon. She chased his mouth when he pulled back, stealing a quick one of her own before he cupped her face with his hands. "And I'll even throw in a sweetener to make sure you complete the job."

"What?" Livvy's voice was breathless, barely more than a puff of heat against his lips.

"A third for us to share," he murmured, groaning when she ground down on his cock, making him hard as steel and aching for her. Rush was used to it. Aroused was a permanent state around his wife. "Carla sent over a few referrals and you can choose whoever you want."

"Oh Atticus," she breathed, her smile bright. "You are too

good to me."

"No way. Not possible," he said, dipping in to steal one last, sweet kiss before he sent her on her way. The sooner she completed this task, the sooner she'd be back with him where she belonged. "I love you, Livvy."

"I love you, Atticus."

Oh hell. He'd *never* get tired of hearing that.

He grinned, slapping her on the ass to get her moving. "Now go and steal the world's most famous painting and break Brant's little security system. You know how much I like to see him cry."

Sign up for the 1001 Dark Nights Newsletter
and be entered to win a Tiffany Lock necklace.

There's a contest every quarter!

Discover the Liliana Hart
MacKenzie Family Collection

Trouble Maker
A MacKenzie Family Novel
by Liliana Hart

Marnie Whitlock has never known what it's like to be normal. She and her family moved from place to place, hiding from reporters and psychologists, all because of her gift. A curse was more like it. Seeing a victim, feeling his pain as the last of his life ebbed away, and being helpless to save him. It was torture. And then one day it disappeared and she was free. Until those who hunted her for her gift tried to kill her. And then the gift came back with a vengeance.

Beckett Hamilton leads a simple life. His ranch is profitable and a legacy he'll be proud to pass onto his children one day, work fills his time from sunup to sundown, and his romances are short and sweet. He wouldn't have it any other way. And then he runs into quiet and reserved Marnie Whitlock just after she moves to town. She intrigues him like no woman ever has. And she's hiding something. His hope is that she begins to trust him before it's too late.

* * * *

Bullet Proof
A MacKenzie Family Novella
by Avery Flynn

"Being one of the good guys is not my thing."

Bianca Sutherland isn't at an exclusive Eyes-Wide-Shut style orgy for the orgasms. She's there because the only clue to her friend's disappearance is a photo of a painting hanging somewhere in Bisu Manor. Determined to find her missing friend when no one else will, she expects trouble when she cons her way into the party—but not in the form of a so-hot-he-turns-your-panties-to-ash former boxer.

Taz Hazard's only concern is looking out for himself and he has no intention of changing his ways until he finds sexy-as-sin Bianca at the most notorious mansion in Ft. Worth. Now, he's tangled up in a missing person case tied into a powerful new drug about to flood the streets, if they can't find a way to stop it before its too late. Taking on a drug cartel isn't safe, but when passion ignites between them Taz and Bianca discover their hearts aren't bulletproof either.

* * * *

Delta: Rescue
A MacKenzie Family Novella
by Cristin Harber

When Luke Brenner takes an off-the-books job on the MacKenzie-Delta joint task force, he has one goal: shut down sex traffickers on his personal hunt for retribution. This operation brings him closer than he's ever been to avenge his first love, who was taken, sold, and likely dead.

Madeleine Mercier is the daughter of an infamous cartel conglomerate. Their family bleeds money, they sell pleasure, they sell people. She knows no other life, sees no escape, except for one. Maddy is the only person who can take down Papa, when every branch of law enforcement in every country, is on her father's payroll.

It's evil. To want to ruin, to murder, her family. But that's what she is. Ruined for a life outside of destroying her father. She can't feel arousal. Has never been kissed. Never felt anything other than disgust for the world that she perpetuates. Until she clashes with a possible mercenary who gives her hope.

The hunter versus the virgin. The predator and his prey. When forced together, can enemies resist the urge to run away or destroy one another?

* * * *

Deep Trouble
A MacKenzie Family Novella
by Kimberly Kincaid

Bartender Kylie Walker went into the basement of The Corner Tavern for a box of cocktail napkins, but what she got was an eyeful of murder. Now she's on the run from a killer with connections, and one wrong step could be her last. Desperate to stay safe, Kylie calls the only person she trusts—her ex-Army Ranger brother. The only problem? He's two thousand miles away, and trouble is right outside her door.

Security specialist Devon Randolph might be rough and gruff, but he'll never turn down a friend in need, especially when that friend is the fellow Ranger who once saved his life. Devon may have secrets, but he's nearby, and he's got the skills to keep his buddy's sister safe...even if one look at brash, beautiful, Kylie makes him want to break all the rules.

Forced on the run, Kylie and Devon dodge bullets and bad guys, but they cannot fight the attraction burning between them. Yet the closer they grow, the higher the stakes become. Will they be able to outrun a brutal killer? Or will Devon's secrets tear them apart first?

* * * *

Desire & Ice
A MacKenzie Family Novella
by Christopher Rice

Danny Patterson isn't a teenager anymore. He's the newest and youngest sheriff's deputy in Surrender, Montana. A chance encounter with his former schoolteacher on the eve of the biggest snowstorm to hit Surrender in years shows him that some schoolboy crushes never fade. Sometimes they mature into grown-up desire.

It's been years since Eliza Brightwell set foot in Surrender. So why is she back now? And why does she seem like she's running from something? To solve this mystery, Danny disobeys a direct order from Sheriff Cooper MacKenzie and sets out into a fierce blizzard, where his courage and his desire might be the only things capable of saving Eliza from a dark force out of her own past.

1001 Dark Nights

Welcome to 1001 Dark Nights… a collection of novellas that are breathtakingly sexy and magically romantic. Some are paranormal, some are erotic. Each and every one is compelling and page turning.

Inspired by the exotic tales of The Arabian Nights, 1001 Dark Nights features *New York Times* and *USA Today* bestselling authors.

In the original, Scheherazade desperately attempts to entertain her husband, the King of Persia, with nightly stories so that he will postpone her execution.

In our versions, month after month, each of our fabulous authors puts a unique spin on the premise and creates a tale that a new Scheherazade tells long into the dark, dark night.

For more information, visit www.1001DarkNights.com

About Robin Covington

USAToday bestselling author, Robin Covington loves to explore the theme of fooling around and falling in love in her sexy books. When she's not writing sizzling romance she's collecting tasty man candy pics, hoarding red nail polish, indulging in a little comic book geek love, and obsessing over Chris Evans. Don't send chocolate . . . send eye candy!

Robin's bestselling books have won the Golden Leaf Award and finaled in the Romantic Times Reviewer's Choice, the Book Seller's Best and the National Reader's Choice Awards.

She lives in Maryland with her handsome husband, her two brilliant children (they get it from her, of course!), and her beloved fur babies - Dixie Joan Wilder and Dutch.

Drop her a line at robin@robincovingtonromance.com - she always writes back.

Her Secret Lover
A What Happens in Vegas Novel
By Robin Covington
Now available!

Forbidden fruit is the sweetest

Kelsey Kyle will do whatever it takes to get into the management trainee program at the casino where she works. So when she's given the opportunity to get a VIP customer's endorsement for the program, she jumps at the challenge. All she needs to do is arrange a one-on-one fan experience with the woman's favorite author, tall-dark-and-intense Micah Holmes.

An entire week at a Vegas romance readers' convention, surrounded by hundreds of people, is Micah Holmes' idea of hell. But one look at Kelsey, his assigned hotel concierge, and the attraction is immediate. Maybe this week won't be so bad after all…

Anything beyond a "strictly professional" relationship will get Kelsey fired, but she needs to get close to Micah to get the super fan experience her client wants. Hot sex in her apartment pool begins a game of "undercover lover" that quickly escalates to something more. But when Micah discovers her secret agenda, all bets are off.

On behalf of 1001 Dark Nights,

Liz Berry and M.J. Rose would like to thank ~

Liliana Hart
Scott Silverii
Steve Berry
Doug Scofield
Kim Guidroz
Jillian Stein
InkSlinger PR
Asha Hossain
Kasi Alexander
Chris Graham
Pamela Jamison
Jessica Johns
Dylan Stockton
and Simon Lipskar

CPSIA information can be obtained at www.ICGtesting.com
Printed in the USA
LVOW12s0350150316

479097LV00001B/214/P